Fur Magic

"The Changer is impatient this mornin'."

"The Changer?" Cory asked curiously.

It was Uncle Jasper that answered, his voice serious. "Coyote—he's the Changer. Before the coming of the white men there were my own people here. But before them the Old People, the animals. Only they were not as they are today. No, they lived in tribes, and were the rulers of the world."

"But the Changer," Ned cut in, "he never wanted things to be the same. It was in him to change them around."

"Only he tried a last change," Uncle Jasper took up the story again, "and it was the Great Spirit who defeated him. When enough time passes and the white man puts an end to the world through his muddlin', then the Changer will return and turn the world over so the People, the animals, will rule again,"

"When," Cory asked, "is he supposed to turn the world over?"

Uncle Jasper smiled. "Well, you may just be alive to see it, son."

THE MAGIC BOOKS BY ANDRE NORTON

Available now:

Steel Magic
Octagon Magic
Fur Magic

Coming soon from Starscape:

Dragon Magic
Lavender-Green Magic
Red Hart Magic

THE MAGIC BOOKS

Fur Magic

ANDRE NORTON

A TOM DOHERTY ASSOCIATES BOOK
NEW YORK

This is a work of fiction. All the characters and events portrayed in this book are either products of the author's imagination or are used fictitiously.

FUR MAGIC

Copyright © 1965 by The Estate of Andre Norton
Reader's Guide copyright © 2006 by Tor Books

A Starscape Book
Published by Tom Doherty Associates, LLC
175 Fifth Avenue
New York, NY 10010

www.starscapebooks.com

ISBN 0-765-35299-0
EAN 978-0765-35299-6

First Starscape edition: April 2006

Printed in the United States of America

0 9 8 7 6 5 4 3 2 1

Contents

Author's Note

North American Indians, no matter of what tribe, have many legends of the Old Ones, those birds and animals (all greater than their dwarfed descendants we know now) who lived as men before the coming of man himself. Some of the furred or feathered people had strange powers. Foremost among them was the Changer. To the Plains Indians he most often wore the form of a coyote, an animal noted even to this day for its intelligence and cunning above the ordinary. To other tribes he was the Raven, or even had the scales of a reptile.

One of his many names was the Trickster, since he delighted in practical jokes and in outwitting his fellows. The Changer aided as much as he harmed, turning the course of rivers to benefit the Old Ones, altering their lands for their profit. His were the powers of nature. And widely separated Indian nations agreed that he at last created man—some say as an idle fancy, others that he wished to make a new servant. Only it did not work out as he had planned.

The legend that the Changer "turned the world over" is current with the Indians of the far Northwest.

One version of the story states that he at last defied the Great Spirit, and through the Thunderbird (that awesome winged messenger, the greatest of totems) was sent into exile. But a day for his return has also been decreed. Where upon he shall come forth to turn the world back again. Man will then vanish and the Old Ones will once more live to fill the woodlands, the prairies, and the deserts from which man has so long hunted them.

Wild Country

It was cold and far too dark outside the window to be really day-time yet. Now if he were back home this morning—Cory sat on the edge of the bunk, holding the boot he was sure was going to be too tight, and thought about home. Right now he would be willing to sit out in the full blaze of Florida sun if only all could be just as it had been before Dad went off with the Air Rescue to Vietnam. Aunt Lucy would be downstairs in the kitchen getting breakfast and all would be—right. Only Dad was gone, to a place Cory could not even pronounce, and Aunt Lucy was nursing Grandma in San Francisco. So Florida was not home any more.

"Cory!" It was not a loud call, nor was the rap on the door which accompanied it a loud rap, but Cory was startled sharply out of his daydream.

"Yes, sir, Uncle Jasper, I'm coming!" he answered as quickly as he could, pulling on first one boot, then the other. With speed, though the buttons did not slip very easily into their proper holes this morning, he fastened his shirt and tucked the tails into his jeans.

He longed to roll back beneath the covers on the bunk, maybe even pull them over his head, and forget all about yesterday. Horses—

Cory winced, rubbing aching bruises. Riding—But at least they were going in the jeep today. Only he did not want to face Uncle Jasper this morning, though there was no hope of avoiding that. He stamped down hard on each foot, the unfamiliar height of the heels making him feel as if he tilted forward, so different from Florida sandals.

Horses—Cory had found out something about himself yesterday which made him drag his booted feet now as he opened the door and went reluctantly down the ranch-house hall. He was afraid, not only of the horse Uncle Jasper had said was old, and tame, and good for a beginner to learn to ride on but of—of the country—and perhaps a little—of Uncle Jasper.

Last night he had lain awake and listened to all kinds of disturbing noises. Of course, he had told himself over and over that there was *nothing* to be afraid of. But he had never lived out in the open before, with not even a paved road, and with all those mountains shooting up to the sky. Here there were just miles and miles of nothing but wild things—tall grass no one ever cut and big trees and—animals—Uncle Jasper had pointed out a coyote track right beside the corral last night.

Corral—Cory's memory switched again to his shameful performance at the corral yesterday afternoon. Maybe it was true, what he had once read in a book, that animals knew when you were afraid of them. Because that tame old horse had bucked him right off. And—and he had not had the real guts to get back up in the saddle again when Uncle Jasper said to.

Even now, though it was so cold in the very early morning, Cory felt hot all over remembering it. Uncle Jasper had not said a thing. In fact he had talked about something else, brought Cory back here to the ranch-house and showed him all the Indian things in the big room.

Indian things—Cory sighed. All his life he had been so proud of knowing Uncle Jasper, boasting about it at school and in the Scouts, bragging that he had a real live Indian foster uncle, who had served with Dad in Korea and now lived in Idaho and raised Appaloosa horses for rodeos. Then Uncle Jasper had come to Florida just about the time Dad got his orders to ship out and Aunt Lucy was called to Grandma's. And he had offered to take Cory to his ranch for the whole summer! It had been such a wonderful, exciting time, getting ready to go, and reading about the West—all he could read—though it had been tough to say goodbye to Dad, too.

He stood in the doorway looking out into the early morning, shivering, pulling on his sweater. Now he could hear men's voices out by the jeep and the moving of horses in the big corral.

Horses. When you watched the cowboys on TV, riding looked so easy. And when Dad and Uncle Jasper had taken him to the rodeo—well, the riders had taken a lot of spills— but that had been watching, not trying to do it yourself. Now when he thought of horses all he could really see were big hoofs in the air, aiming straight at *him*.

"Cory?"

"Coming, Uncle Jasper!" He shivered again and began to

run to the jeep, resolutely not looking towards the corral. There had been a couple of stories he had read about devil horses and cougars and—

The hills were very dark against the greying sky as he reached the jeep. Uncle Jasper was talking to Mr. Baynes.

"This is Cory Alder," Uncle Jasper said.

Cory remembered his manners. "How do you do, sir." He held out his hand as Dad had taught him. Mr. Baynes looked a little surprised, as if he did not expect this.

"Hi, kid," he answered. "Want to see the herd, eh? Well, hop in."

Cory scrambled into the back of the jeep where two saddles and other riding gear were already piled, leaving only a sliver of room for him. Two saddles—not three—one for Uncle Jasper, one for Mr. Baynes—He felt a surge of relief. Then Uncle Jasper did not expect him to ride! They would be at the line camp, and maybe he could stay there.

He tried to find something to hold on to, for Uncle Jasper did not turn into the ranch road, but pointed the jeep towards a very dark range of hills, and cut off across country.

They bounced and jumped, whipping through sage-brush, around rocks, until they half fell into the dried bed of a vanished stream, and used that for a road. Once they heard a drumming even louder than the sound of the motor. Uncle Jasper slowed to a stop, his head turning as he listened so that the silver disks on his hatband glinted in the strengthening light. Then he got to his feet, steadying himself with one hand on the frame of the windscreen, his face up almost as if he were sniffing the wind to catch some scent as well as listening so intently.

Cory studied him. Uncle Jasper was even taller than Dad. And, though he wore a rancher's work clothes, the silver-studded band on his wide-brimmed Stetson, and the fact that he had a broad archer's guard on his wrist, made him look different from Mr. Baynes. The latter was tanned almost as dark as Uncle Jasper and had black hair, too.

Then Cory forgot the men in the front seat as he saw what they watched for, a herd of horses moving at a gallop. But the wildly running band passed well beyond the stream bed and Cory sighed with relief.

"Cougar started 'em maybe," Mr. Baynes commented. His hand dropped to the rifle caught in the clips on the jeep side as men had once carried such weapons in saddle scab-bards.

"Could be," Uncle Jasper agreed. "Take a look when we come back—though cougar is more interested in deer."

The jeep ground on. Now Cory thought of cougar, of a big snarling cat lying along a tree limb, or flattened on top of a rock such as that one right over there, ready to jump its prey. He had read about cougars, and bears, and wolves, and all the other animals of this country when he was all excited about coming here.

But that had been only reading, and now that he was truly living on a ranch—he was afraid. One could easily look at the picture of a cougar, but it was another thing to see shad-ows and think of what might be hiding in them.

Cory stared at the rocky ridge they were now nearing, re-ally coming much too close. Was that a suspicious hump there, a hump that could be a cougar ready to launch at the jeep? Cougars did not attack men, he knew, but what if a very hungry cougar decided that the jeep was a new kind of animal, maybe a bigger species of deer?

The trouble was that Cory kept thinking about such things all the time. He knew, and tried to keep reminding himself, of what he had read in all the books, of stories Dad had told him of the times he himself had stayed here with Uncle Jasper—that there was nothing to be afraid of. Only now that he was here, the shadows were too real, and he was shivering inside every time he looked at them. Yet he had to be careful not to let Uncle Jasper know—not after what had happened yesterday in the corral.

They bounced safely past the suspicious rock, and the jeep pulled up the bank to settle down again in a very rough and rutted way. Uncle Jasper guided the wheels into the ruts and their ride, while still very bumpy, was no longer so shaky. The sky was much lighter now and those big, dark shadows, so able to hide anything, were disappearing.

Save for the ruts, they might have been passing through a country where they were the first men ever to travel that way. Cory saw a high-flying bird and thought, with a thrill not born from fear this time, that it must be an eagle. It was the animals possibly lurking on the ground that scared him, not birds.

The rutted way swung around the curve of a hill and they came to a halt before a cabin. Cory was surprised to see that it looked so very much like those he was familiar with in the TV Westerns. There were log walls, with the chinks between the logs filled with clay. A roof jutted forward to shelter the plank door, and there were two windows, their shutters thrown open. To one side was a pole corral holding several horses. And a stone wall, about knee-high, guarded a basin into which a pipe fed a steady flow of water from a spring.

In a circle of old ashes and fire-blackened stones burned a campfire. There was a smoke-stained coffee-pot resting on three stones, with the flames licking not too far away.

Cory sniffed. He was now very hungry. And the smell from a frying pan, also braced on stones, was enough to make one want breakfast right away. The man who squatted on his heels tending the cooking stood up. Cory recognized Ned Redhawk, Uncle Jasper's foreman, whom he had seen only at a distance a couple of days before.

"Grub's waitin'. Light an' eat," was his greeting. He stooped again to set out a pile of aluminium plates, and then waved one hand at some logs rolled up at a comfortable distance from the fire.

"Smells good, Ned." Uncle Jasper uncoiled his long length from behind the steering wheel of the jeep. He stood for a moment breathing deeply. "Good mornin' to hit the high country, too. Baynes is ready to pick him out some prime breedin' stock."

"White-top herds most likely," Ned returned. "Saul says they're movin' down from Kinsaw now at grazin' speed. You should be able to take your look 'bout noon, everythin' bein' equal."

"Been huntin', Ned?" Uncle Jasper nodded towards the still-barked tree log that formed one support for the porch roof of the cabin. Cory was surprised to see what hung there—an unstrung bow, beneath it a quiver of arrows. Of course, he knew that that big bracelet Uncle Jasper wore was a bow guard, and he had seen bows in a rack at the ranch. But he thought they were only for target shooting. Did Uncle Jasper and Ned still use them for real hunting?

"Cougar out there has got him a taste for colt. Plenty of deer 'bout, no need for him to use his fangs on the herds," Ned said. "He's a big one, front forepaw missin' one toe, so he marks an easy trail. Found three or four kills this past month, all his doin'—two of them colt."

"Should take a rifle," Mr. Baynes cut in. He pulled the one from the jeep clips as if ready to set off hunting the big cat at once.

Uncle Jasper laughed. "You know what folks say about us, Jim. That we're too tight with pennies to buy shells. Fact is, we like to use bows, makes things a little more equal somehow. Killin' the People goes against the grain, unless we have to. Anyway—this is our way—"

What did he mean by "the People," Cory wondered. Did he mean that he and Ned hunted *men*? No, that could not be true. He wished he dared to go over and examine the bow. And the quiver—he could see it was old, covered with a bead-and-quill pattern just like the very old one back at the ranch. And there was a fringe of coarse, tattered stuff along the carrying strap. He had seen something like that in a picture in a book—scalps! That was what it had said under that picture—scalps! Cory jerked his eyes from the quiver and sat down beside Uncle Jasper on one of the logs, determined not to imagine any more things.

"Here you are, son." A plate of bacon and beans, a mixture he would not ordinarily consider breakfast, was offered him.

"Thank you, sir. It sure smells good!"

Ned looked at him with some of the surprise Mr. Baynes had shown. "Cliff Alder's boy, ain't you?"

"Yes, sir. Dad's in Vietnam now."

"So I heard." But there was something in that bare statement of fact which was better than any open concern.

"This all new to you, eh?" Ned made a sweeping gesture which seemed to include the hills and the beginning of the valley in which the cabin stood.

Before Cory could answer, there was a sharp yelp from farther up in the heights, which was echoed hollowly. Cory did not have a chance to conceal his start, the quick betraying jerk of his head. Then he waited, tense, for Uncle Jasper, someone, to comment on his show of unease.

But instead, Uncle Jasper set down his coffee cup and looked up the slope as if he could see who or what had yelped. "The Changer is impatient this mornin'."

Ned chuckled. "Takes a likin' for some plate scrapin's, he does. Wants us to move out and let him do some nosin' 'bout."

"The Changer?" Cory asked, his shame in betraying his alarm lost for a moment in curiosity.

It was Uncle Jasper who answered, his voice serious as if he were telling something that was a proven fact. "Coyote—he's the Changer. For our tribe, the Nez Percé, he wears that form, for some other tribes he is the Raven. Before the coming of the white men there were my own people here. But before them the Old People, the animals. Only they were not as they are today. No, they lived in tribes, and were the rulers of the world. They had their hunting grounds, their warpaths, their peace fires."

"But the Changer," Ned was rolling a cigarette with loose tobacco and paper, and now he cut in as Uncle Jasper paused to drink more coffee, "he never wanted things to be the same. It was in him to change them around. Some say he made the Indian because he wanted to see a new kind of animal."

"Only he tried a last change," Uncle Jasper took up the story again, "and it was the Great Spirit who defeated him. So then, some way, he was sent out to live on an island in the sea. When enough time passes and the white man puts an end to the world through his muddlin', then the Changer shall return and turn the world over so the People, the animals, will rule again."

"Could be that story has somethin'," commented Mr. Baynes, "considerin' all we keep hearin' of world news. Most animals I've seen run their lives with a lot more sense than we seem to be showin' lately." He raised his own cup of coffee to the direction from which the coyote yelp had sounded. "Good mornin' to you, Changer. Only I don't think you'll get a chance to try turnin' the world yet a while."

"When," Cory asked, "is he supposed to turn the world over?"

Uncle Jasper smiled. "Well, you may just be alive to see it, son. I think the legend collectors have it figured out for about the year 2000, white man's time. But that's a good way off yet, and now we have some horses to look at."

Cory's fork scraped on his plate. Horses—but there were only two saddles in the jeep. He glanced—unnoticed, he hoped—at the rail beside the corral. One there—that would be Ned's. Maybe—maybe Uncle Jasper would not force him to say right out what he had been trying to get up courage enough to say all morning—that he could not, just could not, ride today.

But Uncle Jasper was talking to Ned. "Seen any more smoke?"

"Not yet. But it's time. Sometimes he just rides in without warnin'—you know how he does."

Uncle Jasper looked down now at Cory. "You can help me, Cory."

"How?" the boy asked warily. Was Uncle Jasper just making up some job around here to cover up for him? He felt a little sick—after all his big plans and wanting to make Uncle Jasper glad he had asked him—and Dad proud of him—

"Black Elk is due about now. He is an important man, Cory, and he generally stops here before goin' on to the ranch. There's a line phone in there." Uncle Jasper nodded at the cabin. "But Black Elk keeps to the old ways, he won't ever use it. If he comes, you can phone in and they'll send the other jeep up to drive him down. He does like a jeep ride."

"You mean the old man still travels around by himself?" demanded Mr. Baynes. "Why, he must be near a hundred!"

"Close to that," agreed Uncle Jasper. "He was with Chief Joseph on the Great March. His uncle was Lightning Tongue, the last of the big medicine men. And Black Elk was his pupil, made his fastin' trip for a spirit guide and all. He says it's his medicine that keeps him young. Ned sighted a smoke from the peaks three days ago, which means he's on the trail. And he likes to spend a little time at the spring." Uncle Jasper nodded to the bubbling water. "Place means a lot to him, though he's never said why. Has something to do with the old days. He may stay to inspect any colts we bring down. Still has a master eye for a horse. They used to pay him well, our breeders, to pow-wow for them. Most of the old ones believed he could get them a five-finger colt every time. But that's something else he won't talk about any more. Says the old times are slippin' away and no one cares—makes him disappointed with us." Uncle Jasper finished his coffee.

"What is a five-finger colt?" Cory wanted to know.

"A perfectly marked Appaloosa has five well-placed spots on the haunches, and that makes a five-finger horse. Not all of them have it, even if they are carefully bred. They give us Nez Percé the credit for developin' the Appaloosa breed, but whether that's just legend or not"—he shrugged—"who knows. We did and do have good luck raisin' them. And now they're in big favour, for which we can thank fortune.

"So, Cory, if you'll stay here and wait for Black Elk, phone in if he wants to go on down to the ranch, that will be a help. If he wants to wait, tell him we'll be back before the sun touches Two Ears. He doesn't hold with watch-measured time."

Mr. Baynes and Ned had already gone on to the corral, making ready to rope out their mounts.

"All right, Uncle Jasper." Cory stood up. "I'll stay right here."

But as the men saddled up and prepared to ride for the high country, Cory had to struggle not to call out that he wanted to go with them, that somehow he would stick on a horse, that he was willing to walk all the way, but that he could not stay here alone.

Uncle Jasper rode over with a last message. "Don't forget the phone. And your lunch is in a box in the jeep. Don't wander off—this country can be tricky when you don't know it. But you've got good sense, Cory, and I know you can be depended upon not to get lost."

At least Uncle Jasper gave him that much credit, thought Cory, and tried to take some comfort from that. But he knew that he had fallen far below the standard Cliff Alder's son should have kept.

After they were gone, Cory went and sat in the jeep. Somehow, with the sun-warmed seat under him, he felt more secure. He had thought that once the men were gone it would be quiet. But now when he listened he heard all kinds of other sounds. A bird flew down from the roof of the cabin and pecked at some of the crumbs from breakfast. And some brownish animal shuffled around the far end of the cabin, plainly intent upon its own affairs, paying no attention to Cory. But he watched it carefully until it disappeared.

Finally he got out of the jeep, to gather up the plates and pans and carry them to the spring basin, scrubbing them clean with sand. It was something to do. Ned had taken the bow and quiver—Cory thought again of the cougar.

What if it hunted, or wandered, up this way? Would the cabin be a safe place to hide? But if there was a phone inside—

He pushed open the door, wanting to be sure. After the bright sunlight of the clearing, the inside was dusty dark. Cory stood blinking on the threshold until his eyes adjusted to the gloom. Two bunks, now stripped to their bare boards, were built against the far wall. A stove was to one side, a box half full of wooden lengths beside it. There was a wall cupboard, its door open to show another pile of plates, a row of cans, and some tin cups.

In the centre of the room was a table with four chairs. But on the wall to the left, stretched out tightly by pegs, was a skin. Of what kind of animal Cory did not know, but it was large. It had been scraped free of hair and on it were paintings. He moved closer. The paintings had been drawn in red and yellow and black, all colours so faded now that in the half-light he could hardly make them out.

There were horses with the spotted hindquarters of the Appaloosa breed. There were men, some with feathers on their heads, others wearing crude little hats. The hatted men carried guns, while the feathered ones were armed with bows and only a few guns. Cory realized that this was meant to tell the story of some old battle.

As he came out into the open again, he heard once more the challenging yelp of a coyote, and he wondered if it was angry because he was there—that, as Ned had said, it wanted to come down looking for camp food. A fresh wind blew, but it was warmer than it had been at dawn. He pulled off his sweater and dropped it on the back seat of the jeep.

This Black Elk, Mr. Baynes had said he was very old. And Uncle Jasper had said he had been with Chief Joseph on the retreat when the Nez Percé had been driven from their lands and had fled towards the Canadian border.

Cory had read about that. He had always wanted to know about the Nez Percé, because of Dad and Uncle Jasper. But Uncle Jasper had never lived on a reservation, because his father, too, had had this ranch. And Uncle Jasper had been in college when the Korean War broke out, and then he enlisted in Dad's outfit.

Somehow he found it hard to think of Uncle Jasper as a

real Indian. When they had come through town to the ranch four days ago, Cory had seen other Indians. Most of them were dressed like ranchers. There had been just one old man with grey braids falling from under his hat.

If this Black Elk was so old, maybe *he* wore braids and looked more like the Indians in the books. Cory tried to imagine how Uncle Jasper would appear if he were dressed as his ancestors in bead-and-quill-trimmed buckskin, with his hair long, and scalps on his quiver.

Scalps—Cory thought of the ragged fringe on Ned's quiver strap. Had those really been *scalps*?

Strong Medicine

C ory had no desire to wander far from the cabin; Uncle Jasper need not have worried about that. But as the morning grew late he walked along the cliff behind the cabin out in the bright sun. Thus he discovered a crevice behind the spring. Or rather he fell into it, his boots slipping on the rock as he climbed for a better look at the valley stretching on from the line camp.

A small bush that guarded the entrance to the opening broke under his weight, and his head and shoulders were suddenly in darkness as he lay on his back, kicking in surprise and shock. He threw out his arms and they struck painfully against rock walls, scraping off skin against those rough surfaces. As he fought to sit up his struggles grew wilder, for he felt as if he were caught in a trap.

Then he pushed against earth under him, and sat up, facing out into the open. There was a queer smell here and he rested on something soft that moved under his hip as if it were alive.

He jerked away as far as he could, and felt under him fur

and skin. Had he landed on some animal? No, this was more like a bag.

Edging forward, Cory came into the open, bringing his find with him. It was a bag of yellowish-brown skin, strips of fur dangling from it. There were pictures on the bag, like those on the skin on the cabin wall, and some feathers tied to the strips of fur. Though it was shaped as a bag it had no opening, Cory discovered as he turned it around in his hands.

He got to his feet stiffly, the tumble having started all of yesterday's bruises aching again. Bringing the bag with him, he went to the jeep to hunt in the storage compartment for a torch. With this in his hand he returned to the crevice, shining the light into the rock-walled pocket.

Against the back leaned a wooden pole from which hung feathers on bead-sewn strings. And there was a covered basket of woven grasses. Suddenly Cory remembered something Uncle Jasper had said about Black Elk, that there was a place here he visited. Maybe this was it. These things looked new, or at least not as if they had been here for years and years from the real Indian days. Perhaps he had better put everything back just as he had found it. But the top of the basket was squashed in; he must have broken it when he landed.

Cory tried to pull it loose. Inside was a turtle shell broken straight across. And when he picked it up some pebbles fell from it. Nothing was going to fix that again. He would just have to tell Uncle Jasper about it later. But at least it was an accident. And if he put everything back—

He went to the jeep for the skin bag. And he had that

strange feeling for an instant as he laid his hand on it that it was alive in some way. Maybe this was just because it had been warmed by the sun. But he was glad to get rid of it; he laid it beside the smashed turtle shell in the basket, then pushed the broken bush as a cork to stopper the crevice.

Here the overflow of the spring basin trickled into a thread of brook. Cory knelt to wash his hands, and saw the flick of a fish tail going downstream. He wiped his palms on the sun-warmed grass and looked at a tall rock. At least that had no breaks in it, and if he climbed to its top he would have a good view of the valley.

From the jeep he got the field glasses he had brought this morning. These in hand, he climbed to the top of the rock.

The stream from the basin joined a larger rivulet and finally a wider flow of water. Grass grew high and there were clumps of tall bushes or low trees. From one of these copses below moved brown animals. Cows? But this was a horse ranch. Cory adjusted the glasses. Out of the distance moved great shaggy bodies burdened with coarse tangles of hair on their shoulders and heads—buffalo!

Unbelieving, Cory watched the big, horned head of the first animal he had focused upon rise, a wisp of grass now hanging from the powerful, bearded jaws as the bull chewed with satisfaction. One, two, three of them, then a smaller one—a calf. But buffalo had been gone from this country for a long time. They were only to be seen in parks or zoos. Could some have hidden out wild in the hills?

Grazing their way slowly, the buffalo reached the water, stood to drink their fill, the water dripping from their throat hair as they raised their heads now and then to look about.

Suddenly the big bull moved back a length, faced the way they had come, his head dropping lower, horns ready. The other two adults copied him, setting the calf behind the safe wall of their own bodies.

Cory turned the glasses in the direction the bull faced. He saw movement in the tall grass. Wolf?

Whatever was there was certainly larger than the coyote Uncle Jasper had pointed out to him when they had driven to the ranch from the airport. Yet it looked like that animal.

Then—

Cory blinked.

The coyote-shaped head rose higher than that of any animal. It was not a coyote at all but a mask worn by a man, an animal hide over his head and shoulders. Yet, Cory would have sworn that at first he had seen a very large but real coyote.

As the man in the mask moved forward, Cory saw that he wore not only the furred hide about his head and shoulders but that below he had on the fringed buckskins of a history-book Indian.

He did not carry a gun or even bow and arrows as Uncle Jasper and Ned used. Instead, in one hand, he held a feather-trimmed pole such as Cory had seen in the crevice, the feathers fluttering in the breeze. In the other was a turtle-shell box, just like the broken one, mounted on a handle, and this he shook back and forth. He was not walking directly forwards, but taking quick, short steps, two forward, one back, in a kind of dance.

The uneasiness Cory had felt in the crevice returned. He had a strange, frightening feeling that though the man in the mask had no field glasses, though he had not even looked towards Cory huddled on the sun-warmed rock, he knew the boy watched him and for that he was angry.

Was—was this Black Elk? But Uncle Jasper, Mr. Baynes, they had both said Black Elk was an old man. Somehow Cory did not think the masked dancer was old; he moved too quickly, too easily, though of course Cory could not see his face.

Now the boy could hear a low murmur of sound, and a sharp click-click. Cory wanted to slide down the rock, put it between him and the dancer. Yet at that moment he could not move; his arms and legs would not obey his frightened mind.

The feathered pole in the dancer's hand began to swing back and forth and Cory watched it, even though he did not want to. His fear grew stronger. Back and forth, back and forth—now that murmur of sound was louder and he thought he could almost distinguish words, though he could not understand them. And he must—not! That much he was now sure of.

He fought against what seemed to keep his hands holding the glasses to his eyes. He must not watch that swinging pole—With a jerk Cory managed to drop the glasses. He sat there in the strong heat of the sun, cold and gasping, as if he had just crawled out of the chilled water of a mountain stream where he had come near to drowning.

Now when he dared to look again, the buffalo were only brown lumps. And he could not see the coyote-masked dancer at all. With a choked cry of relief, Cory slid down on the opposite side of the rock, glad to have that as an additional wall between him and the valley, and ran for the jeep.

Once more he climbed into its seat, his fingers curling around the steering wheel, shivering all through his body. But this—this was real! Slowly he began to feel warm inside again, and he relaxed.

Cory did not know how long he sat there. But the sun was high and hot on his head, and he was hungry when he finally roused himself to reach into the back and get his lunch box. In his mind he had gone over and over what he had seen, or thought he had seen. Buffalo—three big ones and a calf, and then the man in the coyote mask dancing. He was sure, almost, that he had seen it all. Yet, was any of it real?

There was only one way to prove it—go down there and look. Even if they had all gone by now, they would have left tracks. But—could he?

Cory's head turned slowly from right to left, once more that chill crept up his spine. It was all very peaceful—ordinary—right here. He had unwrapped one of the big meat sandwiches and sat with it as yet untasted in his hand. If he did not go down there—right now—he never could.

And if he did not, then he would have this to remember—that Cory Alder was a coward. What he would not quite admit to himself yesterday after the horse had thrown him, what he had felt in the dark of the night when he heard all those strange sounds, was very plain. Cory Alder was a coward—a boy Uncle Jasper would be ashamed to have around. And what about Dad—Dad who had two medals for bravery—what would he think if he knew what Cory felt right now? Afraid of a horse, of the dark, of animals, of the country?

Dad would be on his way downhill right now. He would

look for tracks. He would even stand right up to face a buffalo, or that dancer with his feather-strung pole and his coyote mask. That is what Dad—or Uncle Jasper—would do.

Cory dropped the sandwich on the seat and crawled stiffly
out of the jeep. His lower lip was caught between his teeth,
his hands balled into fists. He began deliberately to walk
back towards the rock, but he did not take the field glasses
this time. No, he would not sit far off and look through
those, he was going—down there!

His walk became a run as he knew that he must hurry before he lost the will to go and would have to return to the
jeep. He ran with his head down, his eyes on the ground,
with the small brook from the spring to guide him to the
larger stream.

He was past the rock now, and the taller grass whipped
against his legs. All the time he listened for that sound that
the dancer made. But what he heard was just the distant call
of some bird.

Cory dodged about a tall bush and nearly fell as his toe
caught against a root. He managed to keep on his feet. But
that taught him caution and he slowed, made himself look
around. Somehow, even though he was now away from the
jeep, which had seemed the only anchor in a suddenly threatening world, he felt better. The sun was bright as well as hot
and the quiet promised that perhaps the dancer was gone.

He came out between two bushes on the stream bank and
knew that chance rather than any plan of his had brought
him out just across the water from the point where the buffalo had drunk. The water looked shallow. It was so clear he

could see a fish below. And there were some stones in it standing dry-topped to offer a bridge.

Cory sat down and pulled off boots and socks, wadding the socks into the boots. Gripping those in one hand, he jumped to the first of the stones. Water lapped up a little over his toes, so cold he gasped. But the next stone and the next were wholly dry. Then he was on the other side.

There was a clay bank with tracks cutting it. He did not wait to put on his boots, but padded on, stepping gingerly as sharp bits of gravel made him hop, to look at those tracks. They had been made by hoofs, he was sure, though he was no tracker. And not too long ago. But he could not have told whether a buffalo or a steer had cut them.

Cory sat down on a weathered log to put on his boots again. He took a long time, but at last he could stall no longer. There had been hoofed animals here, but would he find any traces of the masked dancer if he looked farther?

He did not want to. But he got to his feet, made himself face in that direction, take one step, then another—

The grass was so tall—Cory halted. That grass was waving, and not because of any wind. Something was moving through it towards the river, towards him! He took a step backward and his feet slipped in the clay. As he had fallen before into that crevice beside the spring, so now he went down into the river, the flood of cold water splashing up and about him as he sat in it waistdeep just below the bank.

For a long moment he was shocked into just sitting there. Then a sound from the bank brought his attention back to the hoof-scarred rise. Yellow-brown head with sharply pricked ears, yellow eyes fast upon him, a muzzle open to show a tongue lolling from between fanged jaws—

Cory yelled. He could not have bitten back that cry. He threw himself away from the bank and from what stood there, flopping back into the river, somehow getting to his feet and splashing on, to put the width of the water between him and that animal.

He fought his way up the opposite bank and ran, not daring to look behind to see if that thing followed. It was no masked dancer; his glance, hurried as it had been, told him that. A wolf—a coyote—a huge four-footed hunter had stood looking down at him. The worst his imagination had pictured for him now seemed to have come alive.

Cory's breath whistled in gasps as he took the rise into the narrow end of the valley where the cabin stood. The phone in the cabin—what had Uncle Jasper said—that someone would come if he called?

Water squelched in his boots, and he found that the unaccustomed high heels made it hard to balance as he fought his way up the slope. He grabbed at bushes, even at large tufts of grass, to pull himself ahead. Then he rounded the rock from which he had used the glasses, saw the cabin and the jeep ahead, and threw himself at the promised safety of both with all the strength he had left.

But as he brought up with force against the side of the jeep, he heard the nicker of a horse. He turned his head to look wildly at the corral—Uncle Jasper—Ned—somebody—

There was a horse standing there right enough. The vividly marked spots of an Appaloosa were half hidden by a brilliant Navajo blanket, draped over the saddle instead of under it. The horse was not tied, but stood with dangling reins.

Cory, panting, turned his head farther. The rider of the horse rested on the beaten earth of the cabin porch. In spite of the heat of the day, he had another brightly coloured blanket folded cloakwise about his shoulders. He was sitting cross-legged and there were moccasins on his feet, the sun glinting on their beading, fringed buckskin leggings showing above them.

The dancer?

But when Cory looked beyond the clothing to the man's face, he lost any certainty. He had never seen such an old man before. The dark skin covering the prominent bones was seamed with great ridges of wrinkles, the chin jutting out in a sharp curve that matched the heavy rise of the big nose above.

Hair, grey and long, had been reinforced with bits of furred skin into braids that hung forward on the blanketed chest, each braid ending in a beaded tassel of yellowish fur. On the deeply wrinkled face were dabs of yellow-white— could it be paint?—that stood out sharply against the weathered skin.

The eyes, which were so hidden among the wrinkles that Cory could not really see them, seemed to be turned on him. And under that regard Cory tried to pull himself together, a hot flood of shame, worse than any he had known before, flushing through him. He stood away from the jeep very conscious not only of the way he had burst into the clearing but also of his drenched clothing.

But the old man on the porch said nothing, made no move.

He must see Cory, but it was as if Cory had to make any first advance. Very hesitatingly the boy moved forward. This must be Black Elk, but what was Cory to do or say now? For want of any guide, Cory finally spoke first.

"I am Cory Alder. Uncle Jasper—he said to phone for the jeep, for Black Elk. You are Black Elk, sir?"

The old man did not reply and Cory stopped. He would have to walk around him to get into the cabin and phone. And supposing this was not Black Elk? How could he be sure if the old man would not answer?

"Please," to Cory his voice sounded very weak and unsure, "are—are you Black Elk?" It was almost, he decided, like trying to talk to Colonel Means. Only somehow this old Indian was even harder to face than Colonel Means, who had once come home with Dad.

"Black Elk—yes."

Relief flooded through Cory at that answer. So he *had* understood! Why, then, all Cory had to do was call for the jeep, and maybe he could ride back with Black Elk and whoever drove it to the ranch, leaving a note for Uncle Jasper. That would work out all right. And he would not have to stay here any longer.

"I'll call the jeep from the Bar Plume." Confidence returned and Cory started on, but a hand of brown, wrinkled skin drawn tightly over bones came from under the blanket and gestured him back.

"No. I stay here. Eat—drink—"

"Yes—yes, sir." Cory looked to the seat of the jeep where he had left his lunch—how long ago?

There were crumbs and smears on the seat, but no sandwiches. And ants were thick about a blob of spilled jelly. Had Black Elk helped himself? No, there was a piece of ragged bread on the ground between the jeep and the nearest tree, as if the food thief had been frightened off, perhaps by the coming of the Indian.

Cory remembered the cupboard in the cabin; perhaps there was something there. At least he knew how to make coffee and fry bacon, if he could find coffee and bacon somewhere inside. He made a careful detour about the visitor, who did not move either head or body, and entered the cabin.

To his relief there was food in the cupboard. He chose quickly: tinned corn, bacon, a tin of peaches, some coffee in a sack. Not much, but maybe enough. He returned to the open, to build up the fire and turn out bacon in the skillet he had earlier washed by the spring. He could not tell whether Black Elk was watching his every move; the old man might just have gone to sleep. But at last Cory was so intent upon his cooking that he was startled when a shadow did fall across the stone where he had set out plates, and he looked up to see the blanketed figure.

Perhaps once Black Elk had been as tall as Uncle Jasper, now he was bent forward and the blanket fell about him in heavy folds, hiding most of his body. Cory, wiping the back of his hand across his sweaty forehead, wondered how the old Indian could wrap up so in this heat. His own clothes were almost dry now, though they felt uncomfortably wrinkled. And his wet boots pinched his feet.

He hurried to pour out a tin cup of coffee and offer it to Black Elk. Once more that skeleton hand appeared, to accept the cup.

"It's pretty hot," Cory warned. But if Black Elk under-stood him, it did not matter, for the old man gulped it down in two long sucks, then held the cup out for more.

He drank the pot dry while Cory sizzled the bacon, added drained corn to the fat, and piled the result on their plates. Then he ate, not greedily, but steadily, not only the contents of the plate Cory gave him but reached out and took Cory's portion also, while Cory was busy making more coffee.

Then Black Elk finished by cleaning up the whole tin of peaches. Cory, licking his lips and more aware than ever of his own hunger, gathered the empty plates together and stood up, to head for the cabin and the phone.

"No jeep now." The old man, who had not spoken during the meal, leaned forward to face the fire now dying back into ashes. The forefront of his blanket fell open and Cory saw what must have been hidden there earlier. Held in his hands, almost as if it were a living animal that must be restrained from escape, was something Cory had seen before—the bundle of skin he had put back into the broken basket in the crevice.

He did not know whether Black Elk heard his small gasp as he recognized it. But he was sure that the other was watching him intently for some purpose.

"Medicine." The old man's voice was thin and high. "Strong medicine." He waited as if for some comment from Cory, and minutes dragged on while Cory felt more and more uncomfortable.

"I fell," he said at last in a rush of words "I slipped and fell. I didn't know that was in the hole, and I didn't mean to break the basket—or do anything wrong!" This was like watching the masked dancer all over again, Cory thought. And he was afraid again—just as much as he had been before.

"You held it—this medicine!"

He thought that was meant as a question and he answered, "Yes, I didn't mean to do anything wrong, sir! I fell, and then it was under me. I—I brought it out in the light, just to see what it was. But then I took it right back again and put it in the basket—honest, I did."

"You touched. Very wrong. Now must be made clean again."

Black Elk held the bag against his chest with his right hand. The left disappeared inside the shield of blanket, to emerge with the fingers tightened into a fist—a fist which was first shaken and then opened over the fire. He must have thrown something into the midst of the coals, Cory thought, for there was a puff of smoke that shot up and then became a column.

"You"—Black Elk looked to Cory—"touched. Now you make clean. Take medicine bag, hold it in smoke, hold tight. You do wrong; now you do right."

It was an order Cory could not disobey. He came reluctantly to Black Elk, accepted the bundle, edged forward until he could hold it into the full stream of the smoke. It broke and eddied about the bundle, floating around Cory's head. He smelled a strange scent, tried to jerk his head one way or another to rid it from his eyes and nostrils. But he could not, and the smoke grew thicker and thicker until he could see nothing at all but its billows.

War Party Captive

Cory blinked, and blinked again. There was still smoke before him, but it no longer filled his nose or smarted his half-blinded eyes. This vapour rose in a straight column to the sky—a signal column.

And he had something very important to do. His hands moved and a thick branch of pine cut across that column, purposefully breaking it.

His hands!

But those were not hands holding the branch, those were paws—with claws and a coarse brown fur covering them! And his body—He was no longer standing on his two feet; he was squatting back on rounded haunches, his hind feet big paws with webs between the toes. Over all his body was thick fur.

Frightened, he tried to screw his head around farther to see over his shoulder. There was a broad, flat tail lying in the dust behind, balancing him as he stood, or rather crouched, before the fire. It had no fur, but was scaled instead.

Cory dropped the branch of pine, put his paw-hands to his face—to touch great teeth in an animal's jaw.

"What—"

He had said that, but the sound in his own ears was a kind of chirp. And he was alone—no Black Elk, or cabin, or jeep, or corral, or horse. Even the valley was not the same. He was up among some rocks with a small pocket of fire before him that was again sending its unbroken thread of smoke into the sky. What had happened to him, and to the world he had known?

Cory dropped down, to plant his forefeet against a rock. Suddenly he felt so frightened he was weak, unable to move. He shut his eyes, keeping them so with all his strength. Now, when he looked again everything would be all right—he would be safely back at the campfire. He was afraid to open his eyes, to take the chance that this was no dream but somehow real. But it could not be! It just could not be!

At last he counted, to fifty, to one hundred, to one hundred and fifty, telling himself each time that when he reached the last number he would look. At two hundred he fought his fear to the point where he could open his eyes.

There was the same rock before him, and the two furred paws resting against it. If this was a dream it still continued. A scream was in Cory's throat, but the sound he uttered was not a boy's cry; it was a guttural animal noise.

Bracing himself back on those forepaws, he tried to look about him once more for some clue as to what had happened. Staring down at his plump body, he noticed for the first time that there were things that did not belong to an animal. He was wearing a band of skin that crossed from one shoulder to under the opposite foreleg. It was covered with small, overlapping scales that glittered in the sun, and it supported a kind of box made from a pair of shells fitted together. In addition, from the outer edge of the shell container dangled short strings of colourful seeds.

By the fire was a pile of pieces of wood, all showing marks, not of an axe, but of having been gnawed to the proper length. And by them was a spear with a wooden haft and a point of bone, sharp and dangerous looking.

That, too, was ornamented below its head with some small shells threaded on bits of grass or reed. When Cory reached for it, he discovered it was just the right length and shape for his paw to grasp easily. It must be a weapon intended for this animal body to use.

But whose body? Not his!

Once more fear churned in him and he wanted to run as he had from the river when the coyote had stood on the bank watching him.

River—water—He must have water! That was safe, a place to hide. Water!

Cory, still holding the spear in his paw, turned away from the signal fire, padding around the pocket among the rocks, hunting an open way through which he could reach the safety of the river. He did not know how he was so sure that it was near him; he was just certain that it was and that he must reach it soon, or a greater danger than any he had yet faced would catch up with him.

He found at last the narrow space that formed a gateway, and scrambled through. He discovered now, somewhat to his surprise, that he did not naturally walk four-footed as his animal body might suggest was the proper way to travel, but that he stumped along on his hind legs, his heavy tail held a little aloft to keep it from dragging, though now and then it thumped against the ground.

Certainly the brush and scattered trees were all much taller than he remembered. Or was it that he was smaller? But he was following a trail in the earth which bore the print of many paws and hoofs which led down the slope.

Water—He could smell it! Cory's shuffle became what was for this new body a high burst of speed. Smell *water?* asked one part of his mind. You cannot *smell* water. You can hear it, see it, taste it, but not smell it. Yes, you smell it, replied this new body firmly.

The trail led to water and seeing that before him, Cory's new body took command, plunging him forward in a dive. Then he was swimming effortlessly under the surface with more speed and ease than he had known in travel ashore. The feeling of danger was easing. He broke surface again and climbed out where a small side eddy of stream formed a pool in a hollow, the surface of which was troubled only by the skating progress of water insects and the occasional bubble blowing of some underwater dweller.

The pool provided a mirror for Cory to see himself.

"Beaver!" Again the word emerged as only a chitter of noise, which he understood. He leaned closer, straining to see, to know that this was indeed what he had become.

Beaver, yes, but Cory's zoo-remembered image did not quite match the reflection in the water. Gauging his size by the trees and the rocks, while he was smaller than the boy

Cory Alder, he was still about twice the size of the beavers he had seen at the zoo. And in addition to the skin strip with the shell box, he wore several strings of small shells and coloured seeds fastened around his thick neck, while on top of his head was a net of them anchored by his small ears. His eyes were ringed with circles of yellow, undoubtedly paint—though why had that not washed off in the water?

He laid down the spear, which he had carried without being really aware of it all through his swim across the river. Using his claws as wedges, Cory pried open the shell case. There was charred moss inside, and from it the smell of burning, around a small coal. He snapped the shell shut again. So he was a beaver, but one who was armed with a spear, carried fire, and wore paint and strings of beads. How—and why?

The Old People! The story Uncle Jasper had told—about the animal people and the Changer. Animals who had held the world before the white man or even the Indian—who had lived in tribes, gone on the warpath, hunted, and—

Somehow the thought of hunting brought with it an instant feeling of hunger. Cory remembered the lunch he had not so much as tasted, the plates of hot food, both of which had been cleaned up by Black Elk. What did beavers eat? Wood, or bark, or something of the sort? He looked around him, wondering what thing growing along the pool side might be best, and thought that he would have to let this new body decide for him, just as it had when it brought him down to the river.

It pointed him now to a low-hanging willow, and shortly Cory was relishing bark his strong front teeth stripped from the branches. He ate well and heavily, intent for a moment on the filling of his too empty stomach. And it was not until he was finished that he began to think again.

What had happened to him, he could not guess, unless he was dreaming. If so, this dream was not only longer than any he could remember, but far more real. He could not recall any dream in which he had eaten until comfortably full, or gone swimming and actually felt the touch of water. Now, though, the fright that had sent him running to the river was fading. What he felt was more curiosity as to what was going to happen next.

Absent-mindedly he kicked some remaining shreds of willow bark into the pool and looked around him. The need to explore was part of his curiosity. He would travel by river, instead of clumsily waddling on land. It only remained to decide which way, up or down.

Perhaps it was a desire to make his travel as easy as possible that sent him finally down. But he soon discovered that the waterway was not lonely. It had its own population, and he watched the life he met there carefully.

Fish wriggled about, and there were birds that skimmed above the water or waded out to hunt frogs. There was no sign of any animal, until he came to an untidy mass of dead twigs and the like wedged against a hole under the water line of a clay bank.

"Muskrat!" Cory could not have told how he knew this, but know it he did. The lodge in the clay bank was deserted, however, more so than if deserted by chance. His lips wrinkled back from his chisel teeth as he tracked a scenting of the story to be read there. Death—and something else—

MINK!

His beaver paw closed tightly about the haft of his spear.

Mink and danger . . . but not recently. . . . The war party that had raided here had been long gone—at least two suns, maybe three dark times. Without realizing how or why, Cory's thoughts began to follow another path. And then, it was almost as if he had opened a door—or perhaps it would be better to say the cover of a book—so that he could read—not much, but enough to warn him.

Mink warriors raiding upriver. And a beaver scout—that was he—questing down. Not in advance of a war party—no. Rather to seek out a new village site because shaking of far hills had opened a path in the earth to swallow up the pond that had held their lodges for a long time.

Mink—one mink he, Cory-Yellow Shell could grapple with—could gain battle honours perhaps just by touching without danger to himself. But a war party of them—that brought the need to go softly and avoid notice. And he had been in the open, swimming as one of the finned ones with no need to fear except from the long-legged walkers.

He raised his head well out of the water, shadowed by the mass of bedding that had been cast forth from the muskrat den. Some of that had been clawed over by the mink; their scent was all through the top layer. And the strong musk of the lodge's rightful owner did not hide it completely. Now Yellow Shell listened and a distant cawing made him tense, very still.

The Changer! Or rather one of his crow scouts. The beaver did not so much as twitch a whisker until he heard a second call, farther from the river and to the north. When he

took to the water again, it was with all of Yellow Shell's skill
and not Cory's blundering. Yet Cory's wondering, his fear,
his need for knowledge was still there, sharing the beaver's
memory.

Yellow Shell worked his way along the riverbank, using
every bit of cover. Twice more he scented mink. And then
another and more pleasing and friendly odour—otter. There
was a slick mud slide down the bank and to that the otter
scent clung, though over it the mink taint was strong as if
the enemy had nosed up and down that clay surface for
some time.

Half buried in the mud at the edge of the water, Yellow
Shell nosed out a broken necklet of shell beads. There was a
spot of blood on its stringing thong. So the mink had
counted coup, killed or taken a prisoner here. He climbed
out on the bank and went scouting.

One otter, he decided. Perhaps young. And the minks had
lain in ambush beside the slide. They had rolled in sage to
cover their scent. He finally found the scuffed marks of battle, two more splashes of blood, and followed that trail back
to the water's edge. They had taken a prisoner, then.

Again Yellow Shell snarled silently. Slinking mink! He
dug the butt of his spear into the soft earth of the bank with
a quick thrust. By now the otter was dead, or had better be.
The mink had evil ways of dealing with captives.

This was no beaver affair. Only mink was enemy all along
the river, for long ago beaver and otter had smoked a pipe in
a lodge they had both had a share in building and made
peace, which had thereafter lain between their tribes. They
were no menace to each other, though both were water peo-

ples. For the beaver liked roots and bark, the otter hunted meat. And sometimes it chanced that they camped together and had gift givings and song dances.

Cory stirred. How did *he* know all this—what otter smelled like, or mink? And those scraps of memory about things that seemed to have happened to Yellow Shell before he became Cory, or Cory him? This was the strangest dream—

He turned his spear around in his forepaws. Maybe if he went upriver again, right back to the place where the fire had been—he could wake up in the right world, stop being Yellow Shell, be Cory Alder again.

Then a shadow swept overhead, making a dark blot first on the bank and then on the water. Again, for the third time, that chilling fear gripped Cory. He screwed up his head, which was never meant to rise at such an angle from a beaver's shoulders. A big bird—black—coasting along—crow!

And with that recognition his fear grew stronger. He was no longer the beaver Yellow Shell with powers of scent, hearing, sight. He was Cory in a strange body and in a frightening world.

And he was Cory just long enough to be betrayed.

Out of nowhere—for he still watched the crow wheel over the river—fell a rope of twisted hide. It looped about his chest, jerked tight enough in an instant to pin his forelegs to his body, and dragged him back from the water towards which he made an instinctive start. The force of the pull overbalanced him so that he toppled on to his back, scraping across the ground, striking the slick clay of the otter slide, up which he was drawn, still on his back.

Before he could gain his feet at the top or make use of his quite formidable beaver weapons of teeth and tail, he was struck on the head, and both sun and day vanished completely in the bursting pain of that blow.

It was with Cory's bewilderment that he awoke again. His head ached and there was a sticky mass on one cheek that his exploring tongue was able to touch enough to tell him it was blood. His forepaws were tightly roped to his sides, his tail fastened with a loop the other end of which was about his throat, so should he try to use his tail as a weapon the movement would strangle him.

He lay on his side under a bush and there was the stink of mink all around. Also, there *was* a mink curled up not too far away, a plaster of fresh mud and leaves across foreleg and shoulder. The warrior faced away from Cory. He had several thongs around his neck, now pushed to one side by the plaster on his wounds, and those were strung with rows of teeth, among which—Yellow Shell brought his front teeth together with an angry click—were several from beaver jaws.

The mink kept shifting position and it was plain that his wound pained him. Now and then he turned his head a fraction and snapped at the edge of the plaster, as if that gesture gave him some relief from his misery.

By the wounded guard's side Yellow Shell counted at least five war pouches, three of them fashioned from turtle shells. This told him that he faced an experienced and wily adversary. For those who counted turtles among their dead enemies were the best of their tribe. As well as he could, Cory tested the strength of the cords that held him. They were of hide, braided, and there was no breaking them. Now his fate would depend upon chance and upon the very important point of how far they were from the mink village. For it was apparent he was not to be killed at once, but saved for some unpleasant later purpose.

It must be, beaver knowledge told Cory, close to evening. And night was mink time, even as it was normally for beaver also. If they went on by water in the dark, his captors might have to loosen him to do his own swimming, and that would give him a chance—

But he was not to be so lucky. The wounded mink suddenly raised a war club, a knot of stone tied to a shaft, the ball having several ugly, stained projections. Perhaps that was what had brought Yellow Shell down. Crouching, the mink listened.

Beaver ears caught what human ones might have missed, a stealthy slithering sound. Then three more minks appeared, as if they had risen out of the earth.

They did not speak to the guard, but half ran to their prisoner, the last one dragging something. What that was, Cory discovered a moment later when he was roughly rolled on to a surface made of saplings still studded with branch stubs. To this his captors made him fast by vicious pulls of rope. Then he was dragged along and dropped, to land with punishing force at the bottom of a cut, again to be pulled along.

Here the drag did not catch so easily, but slipped better behind the two minks pulling it, giving the two coming from the rear little need to lend a push. The sled balanced on the top of another incline, was given a vigorous shove by the minks behind, and plunged on down what could only be the otter slide, to land in the stream.

Travel by land became travel by water, and the push and pull of the mink party appeared to be taking them along at a swift pace. Cory, unable to move, the painful up-twist of his tail beginning to hurt almost as much as the pounding in his head, felt himself borne along on the surface of the river, eyes up to the night sky. Though he could not turn his head far enough to see, he was aware, shortly after, that the first party of his captors had been joined by more of their kind. He wondered if they had an otter in their paws also.

A moon rose soon and its clear light on the water did not appear to alarm the mink party. If they had any enemies in this part of the country, they did not fear them. Perhaps they claimed this whole section of the river as their territory and had long since cleared it of any who might dare to challenge their rights to it as a hunting ground.

Cory was carried on under a place where long willow branches hung close to the water, reminding him that it had been some time since he had eaten. A long—How long *would* this dream last?

Dreams—what had someone said way back at the beginning of this day which had ended so strangely—about dreams? Something about someone who dreamed? Oh, Uncle Jasper—He had said it about Black Elk. Medicine dreams—Didn't the Indians believe that a boy must go out and stay without eating until he dreamed about an animal who was to be his guardian for the rest of his life?

Black Elk—and that bag he had said was strong medicine.

The bag and the fire and the smoke, and Black Elk making him hold the bag into that smoke. This dream had started with that—as if it were a medicine dream. Only Cory was not an Indian boy, and these minks were certainly not guardian spirits out to help him. What he had of Yellow Shell's thoughts told him that they were exactly the opposite.

And what about the black crows and the Changer, who could change animals, and tried to make man, or had made him, and who was finally beaten because he could not change or move mountains?

The ache in Cory's head grew worse. The brightness of the moon hurt eyes that could not turn away. He shut his eyes and tried to put all his strength into a desire to awaken from this dream. Only—how could you *make* yourself wake up? Usually a bad dream broke of itself and you found yourself lying in bed, with your heart pounding, your hands wet, and your stomach twisted inside you. He felt as scared and unhappy now, only he was not truly Cory but a beaver and a prisoner.

The raft on which he was tied continued to whirl along, and he felt rather than saw that two of the minks swam, one on either side, giving it a steer now and then, keeping it steadily moving. Then he heard a distant roaring and beaver mind told Cory that it was bad water—a fall, or perhaps a rapid.

His raft turned in the water as the minks shoved it out of the current. A little while later it was in the shallows, bumping around stones while the war party scraped, tugged, and lifted at it.

"You"—a mink head twisted on a slender neck was held

closer to his so that he could see the glinting merciless eyes of the warrior—"walk. Stop—we kill!"

The sounds were so gabbled and ill-pronounced, it was as if the mink spoke beaver but not well. But Cory felt the freedom as the cords that had held him to the raft were loosened. Then they boosted him to his hind feet, leaving his tail still fast to his neck. The line about his forepaws was grasped at the other end by the mink who had hissed the order and warning, and a sharp pull at that started him on.

It was a rough way, and twice Cory lost footing and fell among the rocks. Both times he was prodded to his feet again by his own spear in the hands of a mink; once he was beaten on the haunches by a club. Somehow he got on, but he no longer tried to think. There was only one thing left, to watch the barely marked trail and try to keep walking it.

They had left the riverbank, but the roar from that direction grew louder. Then they turned again, and Cory, struggling to keep alert, believed that they now paralleled the water. Twice they rested, not for his sake, he knew, but because two of their own company had leaf-and-mud-plastered wounds.

The second time they pulled off the trail, Cory saw that he was not the only captive. Ahead was another wounded, bound with ropes—an otter. But that animal seemed hardly able to move, and two of the minks pushed and shoved him along.

At last they returned to the riverbank and the minks brought up the raft to which Cory was once more tied. By that time he was so tired that when afloat on the water he fell into a state that was neither sleep nor a faint, but a combination of the two.

Broken Claw

A series of wild screams and cries rang in Cory's ears. He tried to move, but he could only turn his aching head a little. And when he did that, he looked into the narrowed eyes of a mink swimming beside the raft to which he was bound. Those eyes were ringed with red paint, which added to the hatred in them.

Beyond the mink's head, he caught sight of a river-bank where there were more of the furred warriors slipping now into the water to head for the incoming party. Then the raft under Cory gave a leap forward as if hurled by the push of a new energy, bumped out of the water up and down over gravel and stones, adding to the aches in his helpless body.

So, still bound, Cory was towed on into the mink village. It was no small gathering place, as his Yellow Shell memories told him that of a beaver clan would be, but a number of lodges.

Sheets of bark had been set up on end, bound together with saplings, all made into cone shapes, not unlike the tepees Cory remembered from the pictures of the Plains Indian villages of his human past. To the front of most of these were planted poles from which dangled strips of fur, strings of teeth, a feather or two. No two of them were alike and perhaps, Cory thought, they stood for the owner of that particular lodge.

But he was not given time to see much, for a flood of minks—squaws and cubs—closed about him. Armed with sticks, clods of hard earth, they struck at him, all the time keeping up that horrible squalling until he was deafened as well as bruised by their blows. But finally the minks of the war party, perhaps fearing that their captive might be too battered before they were ready to deal with him themselves, closed about the raft and drove off his tormentors.

They came to one lodge set a little apart from the rest and sharp teeth cut speedily through those cords that kept Cory on the raft, though not his other bonds. He was pushed, rolled inside, and then his captors dropped the door flap and left him in the dusk of the interior. For it was not yet dawn and very little light entered. Perhaps not for Cory eyes, but for Yellow Shell it was enough to see that he was not alone, that another securely tied captive lay on the other side of the bark-walled shelter.

It was the otter, his fur bedabbled with blood, his eyes closed. So limp and unmoving was he that Cory thought perhaps he was already dead; though why the minks would leave him here in this way if that were so, he could not tell.

Yellow Shell memories frightened Cory; he tried to push them out of his mind. He did not *want* to think about what minks did to their captives; he wanted to get out of here, and as soon as he could. But all his pulling and twisting only made those hide ropes cut the more sharply into his flesh, sawing through fur to the skin underneath. He had been very skilfully roped; nowhere was he able to bend his head to get at the cords with teeth that could sever them in a moment, for the loop tying head to tail stopped that. To try was to choke himself.

After several moments of such struggling Cory lay still, looking about him in the tepee to see what might be put to his use.

Around the sides, except near the door opening, dried grass lay in heaps as if to serve as beds. But the two prisoners had been dumped well away from them. Some pouches or bags of skin hung from the upper walls, far above the reach of his head. There was nothing else—except the otter.

Cory turned his head as far as he could, to watch the other captive. He saw that the otter's eyes were now open, and fixed on him. The otter's mouth opened and clicked shut twice. The Yellow Shell part of Cory's mind knew that signal.

"Enemy—danger—"

Such a warning was not needed. Both the boy and beaver parts of him knew that minks and danger went together. But the otter was not yet finished.

As with Yellow Shell, the otter's forepaws had been lashed tightly to his sides, but he could still flex his claws and those nearest the beaver now moved—in a pattern Yellow Shell also knew. Finger talk was always used by tribes that were friendly but whose speech was too different for either to mouth.

"Mink and—other—"

Other? What did the otter mean by that?

Yellow Shell's paws had been so tightly tied they were

numb; he could hardly flex them now. But he was able to give a small sideways jerk expressing the wish to know more.

"Crows come—with orders—" The otter strained, but the effort was so great that he lay panting and visibly weakened when he was done.

Crows? Cory thought back to the river where he had watched the crow and so had been easily captured by the minks. The Changer? A crow, or crows, carrying orders to the minks? The Yellow Shell part of him was almost as frightened as Cory had been when he first found himself in this strange world.

And, Yellow Shell's fears warned, if this was some matter of the Changer, it was worse than just minks at war. There was even more need to get out of here. Cory looked at the otter again. That animal lay with his eyes closed, as if the energy he had used to sign-talk had completely exhausted him.

Cory tried to squirm towards the otter, but the way his neck and tail were tied prevented him, and his faint hope of having the otter chew through his bonds was gone. If the otter could roll to him—? But he could see that a second loop about the otter's hind feet, lashed to a stake driven into the ground, kept him tight.

The beaver's struggles had brought his shoulder against a lump on the ground, painful under him. He twisted his head as far as he could and saw that the lump was his own shell box. He wondered why his captors had not taken it from him. Then he remembered what it held—the small coal. He had fire, if the coal were still alive. And there was the dried grass of the beds. Could he make use of that? No, said the beaver part of him. But Cory's mind said yes to a desperate plan. Only how could he open the box with his forepaws tied?

Cory began to wriggle, trying to lift his shoulder under which the box lay. For long minutes he was unsuccessful; the box moved when he did, remaining stubbornly under his body in spite of all his efforts. Then it gave a little as he tried harder to raise his weight from it. He did not know how long he would have before the minks might burst in. And every time that fearful thought made him move faster, the box seemed to slide back farther under him.

At last it was free of his shoulder. Now began the strain to turn his head far enough, to roll so that he could reach the box with his chisel teeth. Again that seemed impossible, and so hard was the task that he could hardly believe he had succeeded when he did get the shell between his teeth and held it there firmly. Now to reach the bedding at his left. To move caused agony in his tail, or else choked his throat. He could only do it by inches. But at last, with the shell box between his teeth, his nose nudged against the heap of dried grass.

What he was going to do now was very dangerous. To loose fire where he and the otter lay so helpless—But Cory's desperation was greater now than Yellow Shell's shrinking, and he would not allow himself to think of anything beyond trying to do this.

Those strong teeth, meant for the felling of trees, crunched together on the shell, and he smelled the smouldering coal inside. Then, with all the force he could muster, Cory spat the broken box and the coal in it on to the grass, saw it catch with a small spurt of flame. He gave an upward

heave of his hind feet and tail so that the flame could eat at
the cord holding so cruelly tight. He could smell singed fur
now, feel the burn, had to fight Yellow Shell's fear to hold
steady. For while animals knew fire and used it gingerly,
they still had greater fear than man of what was to him the
most ancient of tools.

Just when he was sure he could no longer stand it, the
pressure on his throat was gone and he was able to bend his
head forward far enough that his teeth severed in one snap
the ties about his forelegs, gave another to cut those holding
his hind legs.

He felt the pain of returning circulation, stumbled when
he wanted to move fast and easily. But he staggered to the otter, bit through the cord that fastened him to the stake. Then,
dragging the smaller animal with him, Yellow Shell reached
the rear of the bark tepee. He thrust the bedding away
from the wall with great sweeps of his paws, throwing it towards the entrance to make a wall of fire between them and
any mink trying to enter.

Luckily the grass did not burn as fast as Yellow Shell had
feared it might, but rather smouldered, puffing out smoke
that made him cough, hurt his eyes. But teeth and claws were
now at work on the rear wall. And before his determined as-
sault the wall split.

What would he find awaiting them outside? Armed
minks? But this time he would be ready for them, with punishing tail, claws, teeth. And he, Yellow Shell, was the better
of any mink or two or three. Even if they jumped him as a
pack, he could give a good account of himself before they
pulled him down.

It was the smoke whirling out with them that masked their going. And the nature of the minks was an aid. For they were of the same nature as beaver and otter; they had to be close to water. And, though the village was on the bank of the river, it was still too far from water to suit the furred raiders. As Yellow Shell made for the stream, with the otter he dragged along, he fell into a water-filled cut running between the tepees. How that had been made was a wonder to him as he plunged beneath its surface and struck out in the direction of the river. The minks did not try to control the flow of water as did his own people. They built no dams, or any ditches down which to float the wood, bark, and leaves that meant houses and food. But this cut was the saving of Yellow Shell and the otter now.

The passage was narrow for a beaver, having been made for the lighter bulk of minks. For, while the warriors who had captured him were much larger than any mink of Cory's world, they were still less in size than Yellow Shell. In spite of the tight fit at some parts of the way, the beaver won through and brought the otter with him.

He surfaced to breathe at last, turned the otter around to brace the smaller animal's wounded body against the wall of the ditch while he cut through his bonds. The otter's eyes were open and he was now aware of what went on about him. As soon as the cords fell away, he brought up his forepaws in an urgent signing:

"To the river!"

Yellow Shell needed no urging. He went under water, keeping one forepaw on the otter until that animal gave an impatient wriggle and freed himself from the beaver's hold, passed him, and slid from the ditch into deeper waters.

Able as the beaver and otter were in the river, yet the minks, too, could follow them there with deadly ease. They would be more wary of attacking either animal in the water, however, where both were more at home than the minks. Yellow Shell noted that while the otter moved quickly at first, he soon lagged, and it was plain that his wounds, which began to bleed again, were slowing him down. One was on the back of his head, proving, Yellow Shell thought, that he must have been struck with a club. The other hurt was on his forepaw, which the otter kept tucked against his chest as if to shield it from even the slight pressure of the water.

A discolouration from blood tinged the water, leaving a trail to be followed by the enemy. Yellow Shell dared not take the time to scout behind to see whether the minks had yet discovered their escape. He could only hope to be on their way in what small time they had left before the hunt started behind. With any luck the burning tepee could hide their escape for a time.

Cory did not try to struggle now against Yellow Shell for command of the beaver body. He only wished that this too real dream would end and he could wake up once more into the world he had always known.

Upstream or down? The beaver hesitated. It was the otter who waved with his undamaged paw that they should go up, against the current. Yet, would that not be the very way the minks would expect them to go—back towards where they had been captured?

The otter signed again, impatiently. "Upstream—hurry—" He tried to follow his own directions, but swam clumsily,

and an eddy pushed him towards the bank. Yellow Shell easily caught up with him, shouldered him on, across the river,
towards the opposite bank. Along that they made a slow and
painful way, keeping under water where they could, pausing
for rests where roots or brush overhung the water to give
them a screening shadow.

For it was day now and a bright one, with sunlight glitter-
ing on the surface of the river, insects buzzing above, water
life to be seen. Yellow Shell ate willow bark within his reach
without leaving the stream. The otter clawed aside water-
washed rocks with his good paw, aided by the beaver when
he understood what his companion wished, and snapped up
the crawfish hiding under such roofing.

He was, the otter signed, named Broken Claw; he looked
ruefully at his torn paw as he gestured that. And he was of the
Marsh Spring tribe, though this was the season when his people split into family groups and went off for the summer hunting. Since he had no squaw or cubs in his lodge as yet, he had
been on a solitary exploring trip when he had been trapped by
the minks. And at that, Broken Claw showed shame at his failure to be alert. He had come upon a slide, he told Yellow Shell
frankly, and had tried it out. Absorbed in the fun of the swift
descent, he had gone up and down more times than he could
remember now, the result being that he lost all caution and had
at last slid directly into a net trap of the minks.

It was not the minks he feared most, however, but the fact
that he must have been spied upon by crows who reported
him to the mink raiders.

"The Changer—"

"What does the Changer?" Yellow Shell asked in the beaver language.

"Who knows?" The otter seemed to understand enough of those guttural sounds to sign an answer. Perhaps he understood beaver even if he did not speak it. "But it is bad when the Changer comes. The world may turn over—as it is said that in time it will."

The world may turn over—that touched another and frightening, memory for Yellow Shell. There would come a day—all the medicine makers said it, sang it, beat it out on drums when the People came to dance big medicine—that the world *would* turn over, when nothing would be as it now was. And all that was safe and sure would be swept away, and all that was straight would become crooked, all that was light would be dark. And the People would no longer be People, but as slaves.

"As slaves—" Yellow Shell's paws moved in that sign and Broken Claw nodded.

"Already that begins to be. You saw the waterway of the mink village. That was dug by slaves, beavers they took as cubs and made work for them."

"And what becomes of them?" Yellow Shell's teeth snapped, his strong tail moved through the water, sweeping a stand of reeds into a broken mass. "What happens to them after they so work?"

"They go, none know where," Broken Claw answered. "But the crows of the Changer carry many messages to that village."

"If the Changer meddles—" Yellow Shell shivered. Again Broken Claw nodded.

"True." His good forepaw moved in a gesture of agreement. "It is best that our peoples know of this. Mine are scattered, which is evil. We must gather together again, although this is against our custom in the days that are warm. What of yours, Elder Brother?"

"They move village. I am a scout for them."

"It would be better for them not to find new water in this land," replied the otter. "The sooner you say that to your chief, the better it shall be for your people."

"And you?"

"To the lodge of our chief Long Tooth, who stays in a place appointed where our people may gather in time of danger. He will then send messages, signal fires, to draw our people there."

"Yet the minks will be behind us now—"

Broken Claw nodded. "The minks, yes. If they listen indeed to the words of the crows and those who fly scout for them in the sky, then we must both travel with the ever-seeing eyes of the war trail. In the water we need not tie fringes to our feet to wipe out the trail we leave, but they are also of the water and they will know." He looked about where they had eaten, and Yellow Shell saw the foolish way they had behaved in their hunger.

It would be a very stupid mink who would not see the stripped willow, the overturned rocks, and not know that a beaver and an otter had halted here to rest and eat.

The otter signed. "Yes, we have been as cubs untaught, my Brother. Let us hope that this does not lead to evil for us."

At first Yellow Shell thought that some of the traces could be hidden. A moment's study told him that was impossible.

All they could do now was to put as much space between them and this breakage as they could.

But while his powerful beaver body had almost recovered from the rough handling given him by the minks, though his head still ached and his exploring paw touched a tender swelling on his skull where the war club had fallen, the otter was less able. And though Broken Claw tried valiantly to swim forward on his own, at last he fell behind. When Yellow Shell realized that and turned back, he found the otter drifting with the current, almost torn away from a feeble claw hold on a river rock.

"Hold this." Yellow Shell took the other's good paw and worked it into a loop of necklace about his own shoulders. The otter seemed almost unconscious again. He watched what the beaver did, but did not say anything as the other made preparations to tow him.

Putting out a forepaw to hold the otter's head so they could look at each other, Yellow Shell signed slowly.

"Where—is—your—chief's lodge?"

The otter blinked. Then his injured paw moved in a short answer.

"Stream—into—river—big stone—painted rock—follow stream."

"How far?" Yellow Shell next asked.

But Broken Claw's eyes were closed, his head lay limply back against the paw that the beaver used to brace it higher.

So, with the weight of the otter now dragging against him, Yellow Shell paddled along the bank, still keeping to the protection he could find there against sighting from the sky. He found that swimming with Broken Claw as a helpless burden tired him quickly, and he had to rest more and more often, pulling the otter out of the stream under some overhang so he could breathe. Twice he cowered in such a hiding place as the shadow of wings fell on the water. Once he could not be sure whether that was a crow or some hunting hawk. But the second time he caught sight of black feathers and was sure.

For a long time after that the beaver crouched over the otter in a cup beneath the overhang of bank, not sure as to what to do. If they had been seen by that dark flyer, then the minks would speedily know where they were. But if they had not, and took to the water now, then the crow might be perched in some tree, watching for them to do just that.

But the minks did not arrive and he guessed he was only wasting precious time in hiding. Yellow Shell ventured out again, still towing Broken Claw. At their next rest, however, the otter roused and seemed better able to understand what they were doing. He agreed that he was weak enough to need Yellow Shell's support. But he urged that the beaver help him now up on to the bank between two rocks.

From that point he made a long and searching study of the river. Yellow Shell did the same, but could see nothing except insects, birds—including two of the long-legged stalkers of fish and frogs. And no black-winged ones. Then below them, a little ahead, the grass parted and a deer trotted out to dip muzzle and drink.

Broken Claw crowded against him, using contact of shoulder against shoulder to catch Yellow Shell's full attention. With his good forepaw the otter pointed upstream and to the opposite bank.

The beaver recognized what must be the landmark Broken Claw had told him about. But to reach it they must cross the open river, in full sight of the sky. And on the other side he could sight no bushes or overhang of bank to cover them.

A cawing flattened both animals between the rocks where they sheltered. Crows—two of them—wheeled above the river. One of the long-legged waders called in return, challengingly, in warning against such an invasion of his territory. Of him the crows seemed to take little heed.

Then the wader took to the air and Yellow Shell did not mistake the purpose with which the larger bird set out to clear away the black-feathered invaders. They fled south, the wader winging after them. But in the time when they had been above the river, had they sighted the two among the rocks? There was no answer to that, no answer but again to make such speed as they could, to get away from that point before the crows could report them, or manage to elude the wader and return.

Bearers of the Pipe

Taking advantage of the retreat of the crows, they crossed the river at once and rounded the base of rock that divided the other stream. Yellow Shell halted in surprise as he glanced up at that pillar of stone. For set as a deep hollow in it, well above the level he could reach, even standing as erect as he could, was the mark of a paw. It was not, he saw upon closer inspection, the track of a beaver, or of an otter, or a mink. Yet it was clearly an animal sign, left imprinted in the rock as if that had been soft mud.

Around it were traces of old paint, and some of that rubbed into the hollow of the track itself, indicating that it was indeed mighty medicine and such a mark as would be a boundary to a territory.

"The paw—" He swam on to catch up with Broken Claw, who was heartened to the point of travelling by himself again.

"Mark of a Great One, a River Spirit," Broken Claw answered. "It is big medicine. If it were otter, or beaver, then the mink could not pass it. But it is for all water dwellers and so cannot aid us now."

The stream, once they were beyond where it split about the pillar to enter the river, was what Yellow Shell would have selected himself if he could have picked their means of escaping observation.

For it was a narrow slit, much overgrown with bank-rooted bushes and willows. Also it was plain that this was ot-ter country. They passed otter marks on other stones, not pressed into rock, of course, as the river spirit had set its print, but left in pictures of coloured clay above the high-water mark. These were not of his tribe and Yellow Shell could not read them. But twice Broken Claw paused by some that looked fresher than the rest and at the second such he signed:

"Many return to the tribe. There is danger—already they may know that."

Again his spirit was more willing than his body. And, al-though he had seemed strong enough to enter the stream on his own and swim therein for some distance unaided, he be-gan to slip back, and finally clung to a water-logged tree root until Yellow Shell once more lent his strength to the smaller animal.

The stream entered a marsh where there were tall reeds and a series of pools. Some farther off were scum-rimmed and evil-smelling. But along the brook the water was clear and Yellow Shell felt safer than he had since his capture by the mink war party. Then the otter pulled against him and the beaver came to a halt where the stream widened to a pool, a pool half-dammed by a fallen tree and some drift caught against that.

At the otter's gesture, Yellow Shell aided Broken Claw to the top of the tree log. Pressing his wounded paw tightly against him, he used the other to beat upon a stub of branch still protruding from the log. It gave off a sound that carried out over the marsh. And then Broken Claw paused, for from far in the water-soaked land before them came a pound-pound of answer.

"They know we come," he signed, slipping from the tree to the water. And Yellow Shell saw marks on the log that said that this signal must have been so given many times before.

So they continued, and the beaver was not surprised when an otter suddenly arrived out of a reed bed, to look at them and then be gone again, giving Yellow Shell only a swift glimpse of a painted muzzle, a headdress of feathers and reed beads. But there had been a spear in the otter's paw and he had carried it as one well used to that weapon.

At last they came out into what must have been the centre of the swamplands, a core of dry land rising as a mounded island, well protected from discovery by the watery world around it. Earth, which was mostly clay in which were many stones, had been heaped and plastered together, perhaps on a foundation of rocks. On this were the lodges of brush, also plastered with mud that had hardened in the sun. The lodges were smooth-walled and wholly above water, but with something of the same look as beaver lodges—as if they might have been copied from the larger homes of Yellow Shell's people.

There were otters awaiting their coming, the warriors in front, squaws and cubs behind, but only a handful compared to the number of lodges. If, as Broken Claw had believed, the tribe was assembling again, not all had yet reached this swamp stronghold.

Coup poles stood in front of about five of the lodges, their battle honours dangling—not strings of teeth as in the mink village, but here bunches of feathers or coloured reed chains. The waiting warriors made way for Yellow Shell to climb up on the island. For these last few feet Broken Claw shook free of his aid and walked alone. Two of the foremost of those who waited hurried to his side, giving him support and leading the way through the almost deserted village to a middle lodge that was larger than all the rest, its clayed sides covered with pictures, and coloured marks drawn in the soft substance and then filled in with black or red paint. As on the rocks some of the marks were weathered, but others stood out brightly as if only recently done. And Yellow Shell knew these for tribe and clan records, so this must be the lodge of not only a tribal chief but one who also held the rank of medicine singer.

A warrior pushed past Yellow Shell to loop aside a curtain knotted out of dried reeds. And the beaver paused, allowing Broken Claw and his two supporters to enter first. There was a small fire in the centre of the lodge and from it came a thin blue thread of sweet-smelling smoke. To one side squatted a very old otter, his muzzle white. As his head swung towards them, Yellow Shell saw that he had but one eye, that the other side of his head was scarred with long rips that were well healed. Before him was a small ceremonial drum made of a tortoise shell with the skin of a salmon dried tight across it. On this the old otter beat softly from time to time, using only the tips of his claws, making a kind of muttering sound, as if something deep within the earth whispered to him.

Facing him across the fire was a younger otter, but one who had yet more years than Broken Claw, or even the warriors who had brought their wounded comrade into the lodge. He was the largest otter Yellow Shell had ever seen, fully as big as a beaver. Around the eyes he had painted black circles, and on his chest hung a disk of bone carved and painted—the badge of a high chief. Thrown over one foreleg and trailing out behind him on the floor was a square of reeds woven together, with feathers tucked into that weaving to make a bright robe of ceremony.

There was a burst of otter talk that Yellow Shell could not understand, and then the chief reached under the edge of his feather-patterned robe and brought out a long-stemmed pipe. With two claws he skilfully brought up a burning twig from the fire and set it to the bowl. With a puff of fragrant smoke rising from it, he raised the pipe towards the roof of the lodge, the sky, pointing it again down to the earth, then east, north, west, and south, finally offering the stem to Yellow Shell.

Taking it carefully into his forepaws the beaver drew a deep breath and then puffed it out slowly, turning his head meanwhile in the same order as the otter chief had presented the pipe.

As he passed the pipe to the left and so into the waiting paws of the old otter who had stopped his drumming to take it, the chief spoke in swift sign language.

"The lodge of Long Tooth is our brother's. The food and drink that are Long Tooth's are our brother's. Let him rest, and eat and drink, for the trail behind him has been long and hard."

The reed matting that was the door of the lodge was drawn aside as a squaw almost as old in years as the drumming otter brought in a bowl, which she set before Yellow Shell, and with it a gourd that now served as a cup and from which came the scent of some stewed herb. The beaver dipped into the bowl and found fresh alder bark, sweet to the taste, and with it bulbs of water plants.

As he ate and drank, courteously ignored by all, Long Tooth talked to Broken Claw. Then the young otter was taken away by his friends and the chief sat staring into the fire, the pipe now resting under his paws but no longer burning. The ancient otter went back to the low drum of claw on stretched fish skin.

But at length he said something to the chief, and Long Tooth nodded slowly. The old otter reached into the edge of the fireplace and scooped up a pawful of grey-white ash. He scattered this over the surface of the drum, adding a second pawful to the first, so that there was now a thin coating of powder on the drum top.

Then, putting one paw on either side of the drum as if to hold it very steady, he threw back his head, so that his grey muzzle pointed almost straight up to the roof over their heads, and began a chant in a voice that was thin, and old, and quavery. But, as the old one continued, Yellow Shell, listening, knew he was hearing a medicine singer of power, one who could control great forces. And so the beaver sat quietly, not daring to stir.

Cory felt that he had been shut tight into a small part of

Yellow Shell from which there was no escape, and this was frightening. Yet with that fear was the feeling that something important was going to begin right before his eyes, and he gazed as intently upon the medicine otter as the rest.

The quavering chant died away and the otter was visibly taking a deep breath, drawing air into his lungs as if about to plunge into water and stay thereunder for a long time. Holding that breath, he leaned forward over the powdered drum. And then he blew his lungs empty, straight over the ashes.

Cory expected to see them all disappear, but they did not. What was left made a pattern, an outline, crude but recognizable, of a bird. And Yellow Shell knew that symbol, for it was one common with all the river tribes, and perhaps with the plains tribes also, though with them the river peoples had little dealings. It was the mark of the Eagle, or rather of the Eagle's totem—the Thunderbird.

The old otter and Long Tooth looked at each other and nodded, then the otter chief signed to Yellow Shell:

"This is a bad thing now on the river. The minks move here and there. They raid, they take prisoners, and always the crows fly before them, spying. Other things move— perhaps they are spirits—but who sees spirits except when he dreams a medicine dream? It is not wise of such as we to look upon the ways of spirits. Yet the Changer is both spirit and of the People, and what he does can mean much evil to all of us. We do not know what he would do. They say that in some time to come he will turn the world over and the People will be slaves if they live. Though slaves to what—we do not know—perhaps evil spirits. Perhaps the time comes now when he would do this. And we cannot tell if there are any we can call upon who are strong enough to stand against the Changer.

"But of all of us the Eagle lives the highest, the closest to the Sky World. And if he will aid us, then—"

What he might have added he did not, for in that moment the old otter uttered a sharp cry. Yellow Shell had been so intent upon what the chief was saying that he had been staring straight at the otter's paws, with only a glance now and then to the face of the speaker. Now he jerked his head around and saw that the old otter was eyeing him, Yellow Shell, with a searching stare.

Now the old one's withered paws moved, shakily, with less ease than Long Tooth's, but with the same authority the chief used.

"The mark of the Changer is on you! You are and you are not beaver!"

Cory did not know the proper signs, but his beaver paws moved in an answer that was the truth.

"I am and I am not beaver. But," he hastened to add, "I am no enemy."

"No," the medicine otter agreed. "You are a friend to us, to all who stand against the Changer. Listen well: if you would find what will defeat him, perhaps make you not beaver-with-another but wholly beaver, wholly other again, then go you to Eagle. For this is a spirit thing and Eagle knows more than we do—or else Raven does, Raven who shakes the dance rattle, who sings the songs-of-great-power for Eagle's tribe."

Cory was eager. "You mean Eagle—he can change me back?"

But the medicine otter shook his head. "Only the Changer

can change. But there are ways, powers, to make him—
sometimes. And from Raven, who is Eagle's holder of spirit
power, you can perhaps discover that which shall be as a
spear for the hunting of the Changer."

"We send a pipe to Eagle." Long Tooth spoke now, his
claws glistening in the firelight as his paws moved. "If you
wish, you may go with the pipe bearers. You have earned
much from us by bringing Broken Claw back, but this is a
spirit way and so not to be followed unless one has great
need. If your need seems so to you, go with our pipe people
into the mountains."

"Yes." Yellow Shell's answer was swift and sure.

"Rest you then," the old otter signed. "For the way is long
and hard. And it will take time for the pipe medicine. There
are songs and dances of power to be used to make it ready."

The beaver was shown a heap of bedding grass at the back
of the chief's own lodge for his resting and he curled upon
that thankfully, so tired that he could no longer hold his eyes
open. But even as he fell asleep he wondered that one already asleep in his own world—as Cory must be—could
also sleep in a dream.

Sound awoke him and for a moment or two he could not remember where he lay, but the dried, sweet-smelling grass
was under his nose and as he moved, it rustled, making him
remember. So the dream was not yet finished and he was still
the beaver Yellow Shell; he did not need to look upon the
paws that were his hands, or the fur on his body, to be sure of
such knowledge.

He turned his head. The old otter had put aside his drum,

was squatting hunched forward closer to the fire. Before him lay a bundle tied with thongs that were threaded with beads of cut reeds and seeds, and bits of feathers. Over this the otter held his forepaws and Yellow Shell knew that this was a medicine bag and one his hosts considered to possess great power. The medicine otter was now drawing forth a portion of that power into himself. He chanted, but in a very low voice, using otter language that Yellow Shell did not understand.

With the tips of his claws, the old otter placed around and over that decorated bundle a covering of skin, pieced-together fish skin, and over that a second cover of woven grasses that was painted brightly and heavily with power signs of coloured clay. Then he arose, with a stiffness that suggested that he moved only with great pain and effort, to place the bundle back in a sling hung from the roof of the lodge.

Squatting again, he sat nursing his forepaws against his chest, singing in a low mumble. But he did not wait for long. The curtain door of the lodge was pulled aside and Long Tooth entered, carrying a long bundle painted half red, half black, so that Yellow Shell knew that this, too, was a medicine thing.

Two more otters followed him. Both wore ceremonial paint and each carried a coup stick that he planted in the earth before the fire on the side where he took his place.

The chief laid his bundle on a decorated mat and untied the first of its wrappings while they all chanted. There was a second wrapping painted blue and yellow, a third that was all red, and a last that was white, each unfastened with great care by Long Tooth. Then there was exposed a pipe.

It was a pipe of great ceremony and a very old one, Yellow Shell knew. Its bowl was of red stone that had been chipped with patience into the shape of an otter's head. The long stem was decorated with reed and seed beads and painted black.

Once the pipe was free of its wrappings, the old otter leaned forward to hold his wrinkled paws over it, giving to it the power he had drawn from the medicine bundle. Cory noticed that he did not touch it, nor did any of the other otters, including Long Tooth.

After some minutes the chief again covered the pipe with the wrappings that had lain loosely under it, one, two, three, four. When the last and outer one was securely tied, he slipped the whole into a case of oiled fish skin, a final protection for the bundle. And to this was made fast a carrying strap so that he who bore it would still have his paws free.

Yellow Shell sat up on his haunches and the grass of the bedding rustled, sounding very loud in the lodge where the chanting had now ceased. The old otter had wavered back to the bedding on his side of the fire and curled up there, as if what he had just done had exhausted his store of energy.

"A sun and a sleep have you lain here, Brother," Long Tooth signed to Yellow Shell. "It is now well with you?"

"It is well, Elder Brother. My feet are ready for the trail."

"And the trail awaits the feet of those who bear the pipe," returned Long Tooth. "Fill yourself from our bowls, drink from our stores, Brother, then go with our good will."

He must have made some sign or sound Yellow Shell did not catch, for the old squaw came in once more with a steaming bowl of drink, a newly culled bunch of water roots and alder bark. And Yellow Shell ate all he could stuff into him, knowing that it was well to depart for a long journey with a full stomach, for that was an honour to the owner of the lodge.

They set out at sunset. The bearers of the pipe were the same two warriors who had shared the ceremony in the chief's lodge, only now their paint-of-ceremony had been washed from their fur and they went with only the sacred white colour circling their eyes, and in bars on their foreheads. Nor did they carry spears, for even the mink must respect an enemy who travels with a medicine pipe, lest raising paw against such travellers bring the wrath of all spirits down upon the attacker.

Yellow Shell had gone to the lodge where Broken Claw lay, his wounds packed with healing mud and herbs. The younger warrior, his eyes dulled by fever, had looked longingly at the beaver.

"I—would—I could—take—this trail—" he signed with slow sweeps of his uninjured paw.

"So it is known, Brother," Yellow Shell returned. "But if this time you do not take this path, there shall come another when you do. Know this, between you and me there is blood shared and we are as two cublings of the same litter."

"It—is—so—and together we shall take the war trail against the mink!"

Yellow Shell nodded. "The spirits willing it, yes, my Brother!"

The three left the swamp by a waterway so overhung with reed growth and brush that Yellow Shell guessed it had been purposely hidden. In places it was almost too narrow for the bulk of his beaver body, but the otters skimmed through it with ease.

Before dawn they were well away from the swamp and had travelled overland, which was the greater danger, through a woodland, heading for a stream that would lead them into the mountains. His companions seemed so sure of the trail that Yellow Shell followed them without question. But they went most cautiously through the forest, sharing out, before they ventured into that dangerous territory, the contents of a fish-skin packet that had sage and other strong-smelling herbs worked into oil, to hide their scent from the flesh eaters.

Once they crouched together in a well-rotted hollow log to watch the passing of a cougar. He was snarling softly to himself as he went, and, though Yellow Shell did not understand the great cat's language, he could guess that he must have missed an early kill and was now intent on making up for that loss. Whether it was the pungent stuff with which they had smeared their bodies, or else the spirit power of the pipe, the green eyes did not turn in their direction. And death on four padded feet went back and away from where they sat in hiding.

Yellow Shell found it difficult to keep up with the otters, though they all dropped to four feet. They ran with an up-and-down humping movement whereas he waddled at an awkward shuffle. And he knew that he was delaying them, though they did not say so.

The forest lay at an upward slope and they were heading in the direction of the heights. Cory found himself listening for the call of a crow even as he had during their flight up-river. At the same time he was aware of seeing more about him than he had ever noted before. To look at things through Yellow Shell's eyes was indeed to see a new world. The range of sight was closer to ground level, in spite of the beaver's large size, but at that range it was much keener than a boy's.

They did not pause to eat; in fact they carried no food with them. Yellow Shell had only the spear Broken Claw had urged him to take, shorter and lighter than the one he had carried before, but with a very sharp point. And his two companions bore only the pipe in its wrappings, taking it in turn with its carrying strap about a shoulder.

At dawn they came out of the forest on the edge of a drop, below which, in a canyon, ran the stream for which they searched. They made their way cautiously down the rise and all three splashed thankfully into the water, the otters straight away turning over stones in search of their favourite food—crawfish.

Yellow Shell was not so lucky. There was only rocky ground here, no willows, alders, or water plants. He would have to hope that up ahead he could find something to fill his now empty stomach. Or else, if the otters were planning to rest through the daylight hours and travel at night, perhaps he could prospect downstream and return.

He signed a question and the elder of the two pipe bearers replied. There was a deep overhang ahead, if the bank had not collapsed. Scouts from the village had long ago established a resting place. As for casting downstream for food—

perhaps Yellow Shell was wise to try. There was little ahead in the way of growing things and he might go hungry if he could not share their hunting.

The overhang was still there and the otters whisked into its shadow, pulling up out of the water to roll in a patch of sand, drying their fur. Yellow Shell looked around carefully, setting landmarks in his mind. Then he plunged back into the water, this time swimming with the current downstream.

For a space there was nothing but rocky walls, and his hunger grew the keener because he began to fear that he would have to go so far hunting food that he would have a long trail back. At last he came out from between those walls as one would emerge from a gate and was in a small meadow-like pocket.

A deer snorted and stamped, startled, as he edged along the bank towards a good stand of willows. But there were no wings in the early-morning sky and he crept from the water to examine the possibilities of breakfast.

In the end he was able to eat his fill, though the food was not as good as that of the otter village. And, having done that, he set about cutting such lengths of bark as would not be too difficult to carry, tying them together with twists of tough root. With the otters' warning in mind, he thought he would do better to carry food with him up the mountain, and he hoped what he could take would be enough.

Eagles' Bargain

When they started on at nightfall, Yellow Shell found his bundle of bark something of a hindrance, but as they went farther and farther upstream, twice having to leave the water and climb around small falls, he was glad he had it. For this was a waste sand of rocks and stones and they seldom saw a green thing. When such did grow, it was only a wind-twisted cedar or the like, which was no fit food for him.

Dawn found them high in the mountains, with one giant peak standing directly before them. The otters, Red Head and Stone Foot, signed that that was their goal and they would have to leave the stream ahead and climb that wall in order to reach the eagles' tribal grounds.

Again they found shelter for the day. Yellow Shell ate sparingly of his food and saw that the otters were following his example, hunting for crawfish, but killing more than they ate and tying those up in thongs of fish skin.

"Where is Eagles' lodge?" Yellow Shell signed when they returned with this food supply.

"Up and up and up—" Red Head replied.

"There is a trail?"

"Part way only, then we light a signal fire," it was Stone Foot's turn to answer. "If Eagle will speak with us, he will send warriors to carry us the rest of the way."

Yellow Shell did not like the sound of that. Earth or water safely under one was one thing. To be borne aloft by an eagle who might or possibly might not be friendly was something very different. But he did not say so to the otters, since it appeared that this was a usual way of visiting Eagle as far as they were concerned—*if* they had visited Eagle before. But if not his present companions, someone from their village must have done so, or they would not be so sure of how one got there.

Again he slept. But this time he kept waking, and raising his head to listen. For what he was not sure but there was a strange feeling that the three in their hollow between the two rocks were not the only ones on this mountain side, that other animals—or things—moved here with some purpose. Though for all his watching, and straining his ears to hear what he might not see, the beaver sighted or heard nothing, save a flying insect or two, and once a bird that skimmed low over the water but did not wear the black feathers of a crow.

If he was uneasy, so were the otters. Twice Stone Foot, the elder of the two, slipped away from their crevice into the water, but not to swim on the surface with a flick of the hind foot to send him driving ahead as was the usual way of his clan. He vanished, diving under with such power as to hide him from sight almost instantly. Once he cast downstream, once up, and both times he returned after a short space, to sign that the river was empty of any travellers save fish. They kept watch on the land, but did not venture from the stream side, napping in turns, one always on guard.

With the coming of dusk they left the water and began the last portion of their climb. Land travel was a slower progress and both the otters and the beaver disliked it. Already clouds were blacking out what remained of the grey sky of evening, seeming to pull in a tight circle about the top of the very mountain that they climbed. Rain came, hard and fast, so that at times they had to take cover as best they could from its fury, waiting until it slackened somewhat so they could cross some open space that provided only poor footing.

Flashes of lightning were bright and sharp.

Thunderbird. His Yellow Shell mind drew a strange picture for Cory, that of a giant bird perching on a mountain top or winging in the clouds above such a peak, shooting those blasts of fire from the fanning of its sky-wide wings.

By one such flash he saw that Stone Foot had smeared mud across his muzzle below his eyes, and knew that the otter had taken the precaution of claiming protection from the earth. Now Yellow Shell reached out a paw to scrabble in a small hollow by a boulder and pick up enough of the wet soil to do the same. For earth stood fast against the force of wind and water, and to claim such protection now was what they must do on this mountain side where wind and water attacked.

At length Red Head, who was in the lead, turned from a last straining climb, and they came out of the full force of the wind into a cup-like space between two rocks, part wall of the mountain, and a spur that shot out from the cliff. Water ran in a steady stream through it, but as the otters hunkered down in that hollow, Yellow Shell followed their example.

The dark was so thick that even his night sight could no longer serve him. Now the lightning ceased and the storm began to slacken so that the runnel of water became a trickle and then vanished altogether.

Yellow Shell had held his paws in that water as long as it had lasted. Never meant for such hard scrambling over a rough surface, the pads on all four feet were scraped and raw, but the water eased their hurt. He expected the otters to move on, but they did not, and he began to think that perhaps this was the place where they must signal for aid into the eagle country.

For what was left of the night they dozed together in the cup, sheltered from the last of the storm, the bundles of food at their feet, the well-wrapped pipe safe between the two otters. But at dawn they stirred, and Red Head brought out just such a shell fire-box as Cory had used to escape the minks.

Yellow Shell looked about for wood. If Red Head wanted a fire they must have some. But he could see nothing save a withered-looking bush fighting hard to keep its hold against a steep slope.

"That?" he signed and pointed to the bush.

The otter nodded and Yellow Shell pulled out of the cup to go and cut it down, an action he did not find easy since he feared starting a landslide that would take him with it. But sharp teeth served him well, and by patient effort he brought down a tree. In two trips he had dragged back all that piece of growth to the crevice.

Just as Red Head had produced the coal of fire to start new flames, so did Stone Foot now bring out a small pouch that he held waiting in his paw. The first otter took bits of branch and twig that Yellow Shell had sheared off for him and with care built them into a tripod of small sticks. It was small, too small, Yellow Shell thought, to last long, but he could see nothing else usable anywhere about them now.

As the clear light of morning finally touched the mountain side where they had sheltered, Red Head set the coal within his tepee of brush and they saw a curl of smoke wreath up. When the first small flame broke, Stone Foot reached out to quickly dump the contents of his pouch on it. The answer was more smoke, but much thicker and darker, with a reddish colour such as Yellow Shell had not seen before. Channelled by the rock walls of the crack in which they crouched, it rose up and up. There was no wind this morning, as if the storm last night had exhausted it. And the smoke trail was like a ladder climbing into the Sky Country itself.

Yellow Shell remembered old tales of such ladders and how the people of under earth had sometimes climbed them, not many finding the Sky Country ready to welcome such intruders. Did—did the otters believe that Eagle indeed lived in the spirit world?

But his companions were making no effort to climb any such way. Instead they ate from their packets of crawfish, and with appetite, as if they saw no use now in saving any of the food for later. Following their example, Yellow Shell finished the last of his now dried bark and withered leaves, and found it not nearly enough to satisfy him.

The beaver had no way of measuring time in a world

where watches and clocks were unknown. But the fire burned itself out swiftly, he thought. Yet the otters made no move to travel on, or to hunt more wood for another fire. Having eaten all their food bag, they settled back again, one on either side of the pipe, as if to sleep away the day.

Yellow Shell was restless, wanting either to go on ahead or to retreat down the mountain. Retreat was possible, for he could see their back trail plainly by day. But the otters were right, there was no way ahead. They were faced with a sheer wall of cliff, as if some giant had at one time used his knife to cut down a slice through the mountain.

A shadow swept across the cliff. Yellow Shell froze as that winged shape wheeled about, circling, and, at each circle, dropping closer to where the fire had burned.

Out of the crevice came the otters. Still guarding the pipe between their bodies, they reared up on their haunches to their greatest height. The beaver did the same. The winged shape came in, to perch upon a pinnacle of the spur that had been part of their shelter.

It was an eagle and, though Cory had never seen one so close, he thought that this one was far larger than the birds of his own world—as were also the beaver shape he wore, and the otters.

It turned its head from side to side, looking down at them, its wings still a little out-held and not folded against its large body. Yellow Shell had to tilt back against the firm support of his tail to see it well. But now he noted that around its feet it wore bindings of coloured stuff from which hung seeds and the rattles cut from snake tails.

The eagle carried no weapon. Cory thought that it did not

need any but its own cruel-looking beak and talons. And now it opened that beak in a screaming cry that shook Cory, and that was echoed faintly from the heights behind from which it had come.

The otters used sign language, taking turns. And Yellow Shell read those signs. They were few and plain, telling that they were pipe bearers, on a peaceful mission from tribe to tribe.

Done with that, they sat waiting. The eagle appeared to be thinking, as if he were making sure of the truth of their statement. Then once more he gave that piercing scream. And, in answer, more shadows flapped down along the face of the cliff, two of his fellows.

The otters, as if this were the most natural welcome in the world, moved out into the open, and Stone Foot made the cord of the pipe package tight to him, using as an additional lashing the thong that had tied his crawfish bag.

Then the eagle who had first arrived pounced, and Stone Foot was borne aloft. A second came for Red Head, and the third black shadow was over Yellow Shell. In that moment the beaver wanted to flee. This was too like real dangers he had known in the past, not an act of any friendship. But he had no time to move. The claws closed about him and with a lurch, sickening to him, he was in the air, the safety of the ground left rapidly below.

There was a vast difference, Cory speedily discovered, between travelling in a comfortable plane in his own world, and by eagle power in this. He closed his eyes, trying not to feel the tight and painful grip of the claws, the rush of wind, only hoping that the journey would be a very short one.

He was dropped, rather than set down, rolling over in a painful half bounce. Opening his eyes, he struggled to his feet—to face what he was surprised to find lay at the crest of that tall mountain.

Perhaps the tower of rock and earth had been born a volcano, and they were now where the inner flames had burned. For this was a basin sloping from ragged stone edging. There was a lake in the centre around an island of stone outcrops. About the outer edge of that body of water were trees and grass, a miniature woodland.

It was the island that Yellow Shell now faced, having been dropped with the otters on a sand bar reaching into the water. And the island was the eagle village, their bushes of nests mounted on blocks, broken pillars, and mounds of stone.

It was a crowded village, and there was much coming and going—mostly of parent birds supplying their screaming young with food. But those eagles who had brought the animals did not stop at the village, rather they spiralled up to the wall of the basin valley where Yellow Shell caught sight of other birds moving in and out of fissures in the rock.

The otters were busied with the pipe bundle, loosing its wrappings, pulling off the fish-skin protective covering. But still the four layers of painted skins were about it as they laid it carefully out on the sand, the bowl end pointing towards them, the stem to the village on the lake.

However it was not from the village that the chief came. He wheeled from the crags, circling down to perch on a big rock by the shore, one worn in hollows where his huge feet rested, as if generations of eagles had sat there before him.

Tufts of weasel fur, for the weasel is a valiant warrior and skilful in evading pursuit, hung from a necklace about his throat, together with the tooth of a cougar, as if he had indeed counted coup on that mightiest of four-footed enemies. He was a proud and fierce chief, more for leadership on the warpath than on the peace trail, Yellow Shell thought, as he looked upon him with awe.

Several lesser eagles settled down on lower rocks. And every one of them wore coup necklaces laced with that which told of their past victories. But the last comer was no eagle.

At first Yellow Shell flinched at the sight of those dead black wings—a crow? Then he saw that this was a raven, larger than the crows he had seen scouting when he fled up-river with Broken Claw.

No coup necklace was about the Raven's throat. But the rattles of a rock rattler were tied to his legs, and he carried on a thong a small drum, hardly larger than Yellow Shell's hind paw. He did not have the painted circles of red or yellow that marked the eagles about their eyes. A dab of white, spirit white, made a vividly plain mark just above the jutting of his beak.

The eagles and the Raven folded their wings as the otters moved with a slow ceremony to unveil the pipe, wrapping by wrapping. They worked in silence, nor was there any sound from the birds who sat in such quiet that they might have been carved of the very stone upon which they now perched. Even the noises from the village lessened and Yellow Shell saw that there were fewer comings and goings from there. Many of the parent birds settled down on the nests, all facing towards the shore and the meeting between the animals and their chief.

At last the pipe was fully exposed and lay in the sunlight. It seemed to shine, as if the sun put fire to the red of its bowl. For the first time Stone Foot spoke, his voice rising and falling in a chant that the beaver, while he did not understand it, recognized as a medicine song, and not addressed to the eagles but to some protective spirit.

When he had done, Red Head, moving with care, dropped a pinch of tobacco into the bowl and brought out his shell box with its smouldering tinder. But he did not light the pipe as yet. He waited.

Again a long period, or it seemed long to Cory, of just waiting. Then the eagle chief moved from his rock perch to a lower stone set closer to the otters. From that he stretched forth his leg, his claws closing about the pipe stem. Red Head lit the pipe, and the eagle chief raised it to the sky, pointed it to earth, and then to the four corners of the world, even as Long Tooth had done with that other pipe when he welcomed Yellow Shell to the otter village.

The chief smoked, expelling a puff from his bill, passed the pipe to the Raven. And the Raven in turn gave it to Stone Foot, Stone Foot to Yellow Shell, and then to Red Head. Having blown the last ceremonial curl of smoke, the otter tapped the tobacco ashes from the bowl and laid the pipe back on its wrappings, the stem still pointed arrow straight at the chief.

A great clawed foot rose so that the claws could move in signs.

"I am Storm Cloud of the Swift Ones, the Mighty Wings."

Stone Foot signed in answer. "We are Stone Foot, Red Head, bearers of the pipe. And this is Yellow Shell, who is—"

The Raven hopped down from his stone perch. Among the eagles he had seemed small. Standing thus on the ground to face the beaver, he proved to be almost as large as Yellow Shell. He moved with a lurch and Cory saw that his left foot had lost a claw. But he steadied himself well on it as he signed:

"This is a beaver, yet not a beaver."

"That is true," Yellow Shell spoke for himself.

"You bear a pipe?" The Eagle looked at him. "Do you speak for the beavers?"

"For myself only. The medicine otter said that the Raven had great power, that he could aid me in becoming all beaver, all other once more."

"But this is not a matter of the pipe." The Eagle's sweep of clawed foot was impatient. "It is the matter of the pipe to which Storm Cloud has been summoned. What speak the otters?"

Stone Foot's paws moved deliberately, giving to his signs the dignity of a ceremonial speech in his own tongue.

"There is much trouble along the river. Those who serve the Changer fly and raid. The minks take prisoners for him, and we know not what becomes of them. Our spirit talker has sung and his dreams have been ill ones. We would know what the Swift Flyers, the Mighty Wings, have seen in the land. For even the edges of the Sky Country are theirs and little can be hidden from their strong eyes."

There was another pause before the Eagle made answer. "It is true there is a new coming and going. The Changer's village has moved close to the place of Stone Trees, though the hunting there is poorer. It is as if they must wait there for someone, or something to happen. Spirits walk by night; you may sense their passing. But to know more than that, we must search—and we have left well enough alone."

The Raven bowed his head in a vigorous up and down. "Yes, yes, it is better not to draw the eye of the Changer, lest he be minded of one. But does your spirit talker fear that the time spoken of is near—that the world is about to be turned over?"

Cory saw all the eagles shift uneasily, their heads turn from the Raven to the otters. He could see that the bold question disturbed them.

"There is always that to be feared," Stone Foot returned.

"So. Well, the Thunderbird dwells yonder. We shall burn sweet smoke such as he loves to have blown into his wings, and cry aloud to the wind what we fear. But also, tell your chief," Storm Cloud continued, "that we shall search from the air and learn what we may. None of those who serve the Changer can out-climb or out-fly us, as they shall learn if they match their powers against ours."

Again there was movement among the eagles as they drew themselves tall on their perch rocks with their pride as strong to see as their war shouts would be heard.

"The Swift Flyers, the Mighty Wings, are great ones, undefeated in any battle," signed Stone Foot. "If this they will do, then all along the river shall know that we will be prepared for any war, if war is what they should bring upon us."

Together with Red Head he began to rewrap the medicine

pipe, securing each fastening. But the Raven turned his attention now fully on Yellow Shell.

"You have come to Raven," he said. "Raven's ears are open to hear what you would ask."

"It is as I have said—the medicine otter told me that if I would be as I was before the Changer looked upon me, I must come to the Eagle and the Raven."

But the Raven was shaking his head. "I hold the calling of spirits, yes. They are sky spirits, and wind spirits, and a few earth spirits. But the powers of the Changer they cannot break. They can only tell you where to seek an answer, they cannot give it to you."

"And will you ask them for me?"

Storm Cloud's beak clicked together in a sharp sound, drawing Yellow Shell's attention. As the beaver looked to him, he signed:

"To do that requires a mighty singing. Such singing is not done for nothing. We have no old peace with your people, nor have we any friendship or brotherhood with you, Beaver-who-is-not-wholly-a-beaver."

"Friendship is a matter of giving as well as taking." The Yellow Shell part of him made a bolder answer than Corey might have used. "I ask not to be given where I do not give. What would you want of me as a price for such a singing?"

The Raven did not answer; it was as if he believed this a matter of bargaining between Yellow Shell and the chief. He himself was content upon Storm Cloud's decision.

"You are of those who master water," the Eagle said after a long moment's pause. He might have been trying to determine some manner of payment of benefit to his tribe, thought Corey. "This, our lake, is sometimes too full. Rocks tumble from the cliffs and close the stream that empties it, and then there is much hard labour to clear them free. Twice have storms so filled it that lower nests have been washed away. Dig you a way for water to run, one that we may use at such times, and this singing shall be yours."

"I am but one beaver," Yellow Shell countered. "This may be such a task as would need a whole clan to do."

Storm Cloud's bill clicked again, impatiently. "A whole clan does not ask for spirit singing, but you do. Therefore it is your task. And perhaps only you can find a way to use the stream that is, clear it more easily of rocks."

"What I can do, I shall," Yellow Shell promised.

The otters had the pipe recovered, were ready to be gone, and Storm Cloud had already assigned two of his warriors to fly them down the mountain. But Yellow Shell had a few moments to talk with them. He signed a wish that they might find his own people and warn them against marching south into these river lands where trouble was gathering. And this, Red Head agreed, they would do, sending their best scout north. Then the otters were snatched up by the eagles, who seemed to want to rid themselves of their guests as soon as possible, and Yellow Shell was left behind.

Storm Cloud, too, was a-wing, heading back to the crags, and only a young eagle swooped about the beaver. Even as Raven signed, "Split Bill will show you the waterway," the eagle's clutch was hard upon him, and he, too, was borne skyward in a fearsome soaring.

Raven's Sing

Yellow shell looked over the terrain when the eagle warrior dropped him at the outlet of the lake. There was a stream that fed through a narrow gap and the beaver could see how a fall of rocks from above would dam it. But this was not a trouble his people had had to face before, for their task was usually the making, not the clearing, of dams.

He swam along the river outlet, nosing at both banks, trying to find some way to deepen the flow of water. But he could not see any method of tunnelling through the stone of the cliffs.

Since the present outlet was so banked with rock, he returned to the lake and began to explore its banks at this end. The eagle who had brought him grew bored and flew away, and Yellow Shell was left alone to face what seemed a hopeless task. But the beaver stubbornly refused to admit defeat.

In the end his forelegs and head suddenly broke through a screen of brush into a hole in the mountain cup. If all the basin had been formed by a volcano in action, then this crack had come at that time, with a later spread of molten rock to roof above it. When Yellow Shell padded into it, he found not the crevice he had first expected but a channel, which brought him, by a very dark way, out on the open mountain side on the other side of the basin wall.

He went back to the valley of the lake and squatted down at the edge of the water, eating a hearty meal of freshly stripped bark while he studied the bank by that fissure. It was a big job for one beaver working alone, but he could see no other possible way to provide the eagles' lake with an emergency overflow exit. By mid-afternoon he was at work.

The bank of the lake must be undermined, cut through so that there was an open spillway into that crack. He dug with his forepaws until they were as sore as they had been from travel over stone. Rocks had to be loosened and pushed from side to side, then firmly embedded again to make a kind of funnel into the spillway.

He worked through the last of the daylight, keeping on into the night, stopping only now and then for a much needed rest or to eat again from the food about him. Now he had a raw gash in the earth, partly walled in with stones and such pieces of hard saplings as he could pound and wedge in for security. Mud mixed with broken brush was then plastered over that foundation, all to form a channel. The whole thing was the height of his body above the present level of the lake, and at that end he built another wall of small stones, to be easily shifted by the strong claws of the eagles when the need arose.

He was lying with his sore feet in the lapping waters of the lake at the next sunrise, so tired he thought that he could not easily move again. But to the best of his beaver skill he had provided the eagles with the safety they needed. Let the river leading from the lake again be sealed by falling stones and they need only pull out the thin dam corking this outlet, and the flood would pour through the new channel. Of course there was no way of testing it until such a calamity occurred, and Yellow Shell wondered dully if they would demand such proof before they fulfilled their part of the bargain.

There was the whir of wings in the air above him and the eagle who had brought him there, or one enough like him to be his twin, landed on the edge of the restraining dam Yellow Shell had built. He teetered there as he looked down into the channel the beaver had cut and walled.

Yellow Shell was too tired to lift his paws in any language sign. But he nodded, first to the lake and then to the spillway he had made, hoping that the eagle, if he were a messenger, would understand that the task was done.

The bird's sharp eyes shifted from the animal to the cut leading to the dark hole in the basin side. Then his claws formed a series of signs.

"This is a way through the rock?"

Yellow Shell pulled his sore paws from the soothing water to sign back:

"A way through the mountain wall. When the water rises, pull the stones now under you. There will be a new way to drain—"

The eagle bent his head to survey the dam on which he perched, touched his beak to one of the topmost stones as if testing its stability, or else estimating his chance of being able to move it when the need arose. Apparently he was satisfied, for without another sign to Yellow Shell he took wing and was out over the lake in a couple of sweeps, heading, the beaver noted, not for the village on the island but up to the crags where Storm Cloud and his escort of warriors had gone the day before.

Yellow Shell combed at his muddy fur, wincing when his sore paw hurt, but intent on making himself clean if the eagles were to come to inspect his handiwork. Their pride was known to all the tribes, but the beavers were certainly not the least among the People. He wished he had his boxes of paint, his ceremonial beads and belt, that he might make a proper showing. For, looking at his work of the past hours, he thought he could take pride in it.

The eagle who had come to inspect did serve as a messenger, for more mighty wings were visible in the morning air and very shortly Storm Cloud, together with those who must be his subchiefs and leading warriors, settled on the dam. They looked at the dam, at the cut behind it, at the crevice into which the waters would be funnelled when the need arose. Yellow Shell signed to the eagle chief the purpose of each part of the spillway.

Now—would the eagles demand from him a demonstration—one which would mean that he must somehow dam that other river outlet and turn the water into this? At the very thought of such labour, his paws burned and his back ached. But it would appear that Storm Cloud was not so suspicious of the beaver's skill.

The eagle chief himself walked along the now dry funnel, thrust his head and shoulders well into the hole of the crevice. But he did not go all the way through. Perhaps he could see the light at the other end, which was now more visible since Yellow Shell had also cleaned the exit to allow easy passage.

The eagle chief came back to face the beaver.

"It is well," he signed. "You have made what was needed. Therefore we shall now do as we promised."

He must have given some signal that Yellow Shell was not aware of, for one of the waiting warriors suddenly caught the beaver and rose into the air. Yellow Shell closed his eyes against that fear of being so far from the safe ground and hung motionless in his bearer's hold as the wind blew chill about him.

They did not return to the shore across from the village island where he and the otters had been deposited before. Rather they climbed up to the crags from which Storm Cloud had come. Here was a flat shelf on which the beaver was dropped and he sat carefully as close to its middle as he could without his distrust of these heights being visible to his hosts—or so he hoped.

The rock about him was cracked and broken and these holes and crevices seemed to serve the birds as lodges. One such opening faced Yellow Shell now. They were all patterned with drawings to celebrate coups and deeds, not only of the living warriors who now inhabited them but those of their ancestors, for the eagles must have lived here a long, long time. But the lodge of stone that Yellow Shell faced was very different from the others in that its painted border was all of pictures showing strong medicine. And, as Yellow Shell hunched there looking at those, Raven hopped forth from the crack of the doorway. He clapped his wings vigor-

ously and, at his summons, two young eagles came from behind him, one carrying a small drum painted half red, half
white, the other a bundle that he put down carefully beside a
spot on the rock stained black by many past fires.

The eagle who had brought out the bundle now went to
one side, pulling back to the fire site in three or four trips
short lengths of well-dried wood that he built up into a tepee
shape. This done, he went to perch with the other eagles, except for the one with the drum. There were rocks for their
sitting all around the open space. Yellow Shell turned his
head from right to left and saw that all the birds had settled
down quietly in a ring, though he did not turn his back on
Raven to see if they were also behind him.

Now the drummer began to thump with the claws of his
right foot, first gently, then with more force, so that it
sounded at the beginning as might the mutter of thunder as
yet far off, growing stronger and stronger.

Raven took a coal from a firebox, set it to the tepee of
wood, tossing into the flames that followed substances he
took from his bundles.

Smoke came, and it was coloured, first blue, then red—
and there was a mingling of strange odours to be sniffed.
The puffs of smoke did not spread, but rose in a smooth,
straight pillar to the clouds as had the signal fire of the otters. Yellow Shell, straining back his head on his thick neck
to watch them climb, thought that this looked more and
more like a rope reaching to the Sky Country—which, here
on the mountain top, could not be too far away.

Was Raven planning to use that to reach the Sky World
and talk there with the spirit peoples?

It would seem not. Once the smoke was thick and climbing well, Raven fastened dance rattles to his feet, took up turtle shells filled with pebbles. Then he began to dance about the fire, and as he danced he sang, though the words he croaked had no meaning for Yellow Shell.

Tired as he was, the beaver tried to fight sleep; yet in spite of all his efforts, his head would nod forward on his chest and his eyes close. Then he would straighten up with a start, glancing around hurriedly to see if the eagles or Raven had noticed.

But they were watching only Raven. Finally the fight became too much for Yellow Shell and there was a moment when he did not wake again, but went further into sleep.

And he dreamed, knowing even as he dreamed that this was a spirit dream and one he must remember when he awakened.

He was flying high in the sky, not borne so by one of the eagles so that the dread of falling was ever with him, but as if he, too, had wings and had worn them all his life.

Below him stretched all the world as was known to Yellow Shell. There was the lake from which his clan had begun their march south. And he saw them now, recognizing each and every one of them. They had an otter in their midst and were watching that animal's flying forepaws. So Yellow Shell knew that the warning against the south had reached them and they would now turn back, or perhaps east or west, to safety.

And he saw the river, and the swamp marsh of the otter village where warriors now made new spears and squaws were working on a mighty gathering of food, as if they thought that their island home might be under siege.

There, too, was the mink lodge where he and Broken Claw had been held captive, and there he saw the minks lashing beaver slaves, thin, worn, undersized, to work building new canals. And Yellow Shell ground his teeth together in hot anger at the sight.

But all this was not what the spirits wished him to see. He was swept along, rather than flew, to the southeast, with the mountains of the eagles now at his back. So he came to a land that was prairie, changing to desert in places. There was a village and he saw that it was one of the coyotes, and now he knew that what he was to be shown was the stronghold of the Changer.

Down and down he dropped over that village, until he feared that any one of those there would raise head to the sky and see him. But none did, for the spirit dream was his protection. And he came to ground before a skin-walled lodge set a little apart from the rest. On it were pictures of great and strong medicine, so that he feared to put out a paw to raise the flap of the doorway. Yet that he must do, for the need that had brought him there so ordered him.

Thus he came into the lodge and recognized it for one of a great medicine person. But the spirits of his dreams raised his eyes to the centre pole of the lodge and to the bundle hanging there, and he knew that this was what he must have for his own if he would be only Yellow Shell again. But when he reached up his forepaws to seize it, there was a billow of dark and stinking smoke from the place of fire and he leaped back, a leap that took him through the door flap into the open again. Then he found that he could not return, rather he was again soaring into the air, heading away from the coyote town, back to the eagle mountain. And at last he sat in the rock crags, across the smoking fire from Raven, who no longer danced. The drumming had stopped and the drummer was gone, so were the eagles who had watched. It was the beginning of night.

"You know," Raven did not sign that but croaked the words in beaver, which, though harshly accented, were plain enough for Yellow Shell to understand.

"Yes, I know," the beaver returned.

"To that place you must go, and the medicine bundle you must take, then shall you be able to force the Changer to make the wrong once more right. For that bundle is his strength and without it he is but half of what he wants to be."

"A long way," Yellow Shell said. "It will take much time."

"Not too long by wing," Raven replied briskly. "Four feet would make much of it, but we shall do better for you."

"You are kind—"

Raven opened his beak in harsh laughter. "I do not do this for kindness, Beaver. I do it because the Changer and I have old troubles between us. Once we were friends and made medicine together. Then he learned secretly that which he would not share with me, and he walked apart, daring to laugh when I asked that we should do as brothers and have no knowledge held one from the other. Thus, bring the Changer to humbleness and I shall be glad. I would ask you for his medicine, but the spirits have foretold that that must serve another purpose. However, without it he shall suffer and that shall be as I wish it."

He got up and the dance rattles about his feet gave off a faint whisper of sound.

"I cannot ask you into my lodge, Beaver, for there is much there that only I can safely look upon. But you will find shelter in that crevice over there, and food. Rest for a time, and then there shall come one to see you on the first part of your journey."

Yellow Shell crawled out of the wind, which now blew very chill about him, into the opening Raven had pointed to. There he found some bark one of the eagles must have brought from below. It was not what he would have chosen for himself, and it tasted bitter. But he ate it thankfully and curled up to sleep.

Before there was any light a clawed foot shook him awake. It was the young eagle drummer who stood over him. Seeing Yellow Shell's eyes open, he signed swiftly that they must go. He did not give the beaver any time to protest or question, but, as soon as Yellow Shell crawled from the crevice, he seized him, and they were off into the dark clouds and the wind. For the third time that flight was a frightening thing and the beaver shut his eyes to endure it. To make it worse, this was a longer flight than that up the mountain or to the end of the lake. Those now seemed to have been only short moments of danger.

Over him the powerful wings beat steadily and Yellow Shell guessed that, as in the spirit dream, they were heading southwest, away from the mountains and over the prairie desert land where he had seen the coyote village. He tried to think what he would do when he got there. To secure such a precious thing from the lodge where it was hung, in the midst of an enemy village, was so dangerous an undertaking that he could not hope to be successful. Yet the spirit dream had made most clear that that he must do.

Suddenly he guessed that the eagle was descending and he opened his eyes. Being held as he was face downward, he could indeed see the earth racing up to meet him. But morning could not be too far distant as the light was now grey—yet it was still dark and shadowed on the ground.

The eagle did not set him down gently, but loosed his grip, so that Yellow Shell fell into the midst of a bush and was fighting against its thorned branches all in an instant. When he had battled his way free of that, his bearer was only a very distant moving object in the sky, and he had no chance to thank him, if one could truly offer thanks for being dumped so unceremoniously in an unknown land, perhaps very near an enemy village.

Yellow Shell sat up on his haunches and looked about. This was plainly open prairie land and not too rich, for the only bushes he could see were stubby ones with a starved look as if good soil and much water were things they had never known since their seeding. There were patches of bare sand here and there that gave rooting to nothing at all.

He turned his head slowly. The coyote village, wherever it might lie, could not be set too far from some source of water, for water all animals must have. Now he sniffed each puff of wind that reached him, drew in deep breaths in every direction, hoping to pick up the scent of water.

Not only must he find water as a probable guide to the village but as a source of food. The withered stuff the eagles had supplied the night before had blunted his hunger, but it had not really satisfied him, and now he wanted, needed food, and must have it.

He was facing south when the very faint scent he hunted reached him. There was no help for it, he must walk, over a country that was not meant for his kind, awkward and slow on land. His only hope of ever reaching that water was to be always alert to all that lay about him.

The sun was rising as he thumped along, his paws beginning to hurt again as they met the hot, hard surface. He kept when he could to the patches of coarse grass that offered cushioning. There was life here; he saw birds, a lizard or two out in the early morning before heat drove them into cover. And once he made a wide circle around a place where the hated, musky scent of snake was a warning.

His only relief was that the odour of water grew ever stronger, drawing him forward with longing to plunge into some river, even into a pool, with cool wet all about him. Then he stiffened and crouched low in the shadow of a bush, hoping he had taken to that cover in time. The loud, ear-hurting call of a crow, of more than one, sounded clearly across the land.

Turning his head up and back, Yellow Shell was able to sight them as they passed overhead—three of them, south-bound as himself but angling a little more to the east. If he dared believe they were on their way to the coyote village, then there was a hope that he could still reach water some distance away from the enemy, for the scent seemed to run from east to west.

Making very sure that the crows were well away before he left his bush shelter, Yellow Shell stumbled on. He marked ahead every bush or stand of tall grass in which he could crouch if the need for hiding arose, and he made the best speed he could in a zigzag path from one to the next.

The water scent was so strong now that he had a hard time keeping from breaking into a run. But he held to his caution and kept up his move from cover to cover, waiting in between times. The sun was growing hotter and there were more birds, but no lizards, to be seen. Once he sighted a pair of rabbits. They were painted for a raid, and were moving with caution like him. Young bucks, he thought, perhaps out in a daring attempt to count some coup in coyote country—though he thought that their daring was that of young fools and that any coups counted in that way should be their shame and not their glory.

Beavers counted bravery a virtue as much as any other of the People, but a brave fool got no praise from them for his folly. Yellow Shell kept carefully out of sight of the pair, when in other times he might have asked for directions. If they did fall to the coyotes, which was only too possible, he wanted no tales told about his presence in a place where a lone beaver could be so noteworthy a happening as to attract instant attention and investigation.

The ground suddenly ended in a sharp-edged drop and he looked down into a gully. Perhaps at other times of the year the stream at the bottom of it was a sizable river. But now it had shrunk into hardly more than a series of pools, all shallow—too much so, at least the ones he saw, for swimming. But it was water and his whole body longed for its touch.

Only the gully was so open. To venture down there where

there was no shelter was only asking to be sighted by crows, by any coyote on scout.

Yellow Shell angled along the bank, looking longingly at the pools that at another time would have disgusted him by the murkiness of their water. As he went, the pools did grow larger and joined with one another, and there were actually signs of a sluggish current. Perhaps closer to the source of this dying river there was more water.

At last he caught sight of greenery growing in the gully and, with a thankful sigh of relief, he half tumbled over the edge, to slip and roll down to the stream's edge. But he was not so forgetful of danger not to turn and hide as much of the signs of his passing as he could by wide sweeps of his tail.

The growth was scrub alder and he feasted upon it. But he was careful to take his twigs and bark from spots where the breakage would not be easily seen. And he also cut a small bundle for future use as he had before they had climbed the mountain. In a semidesert land one could not depend on too much to be found.

There was one pool that gave him a chance to sink deep beneath the surface, wet through his sand- and soil-burdened fur, ease the smarting of his paws. He dove and swam, always staying in the shadow the growth threw across the water, until he felt almost his old strong self again.

By the measurement of the sun's path, it was now past noon. He half floated on the water, trying to plan. As with most of the People, the coyotes preferred the night to the bright of day. And dark would find their camp alert and awake. To push on now for a first look around, if the village did not lie too far ahead, might be wise. He tightened the reeds binding his bundle of food and began to swim, taking to the bank again only when the water grew too shallow. But there were not many such places now. In fact the stream soon became a river instead of a series of pools, and he was able to make faster time than he had all the earlier part of this day.

A Forest of Stone

It was sunset, the sun having already dropped behind the mountains to the west. Yellow Shell crouched in a thicket while he rubbed vigorously into his coarse upper fur pawfuls of bruised, strongly scented leaves. His hope that this might cover his own musky odour was perhaps wrong, but it was the only protection he now had. And to get into the coyote camp, to that lodge that stood just a little apart but was the same one he had seen in the spirit dream, was now necessary.

He had watched it for a long time. But the door flap had remained down, whereas those in the others of the camp were propped open, lashed to small sticks to keep them so. This could mean one of two things—that the lodge was indeed empty, or that its owner was at home and desired no visitors. And for the beaver's purpose there was a vast difference between those two facts.

It had been late afternoon when he had found the village on the north side of the shallow river. On the south bank were more patches of sand until the land began to be true desert country.

Yellow Shell had not had much time for exploring or scouting the camp, for the coyotes were already stirring. Young squaws came down to the water's edge, bringing skin bags rubbed with fat to make them water-tight, taking the liquid back to their tepees. Cubs ran about, playing wild pounce and chase games. And the beaver watched yawning warriors come out of their lodges, stretch, grimace to show long fangs, snap at flies, rouse for the night's hunting hours. He wondered then about the two rabbit braves—would they be caught in this territory before they could retreat?

One coyote, or two, or even three, he would dare to face by himself. His teeth, his tail, his spear were deadly weapons. But to be set upon by a pack—that would be like the ambush of the minks all over again. So Yellow Shell prudently withdrew downriver into hiding, to consider what must be done.

He might, of course, go into hiding to wait out the night, try to reach the lodge again the next morning when the village was once more asleep. But time was important. He could not be sure how he knew that, only that it was so.

There was this—he could watch for his chance, and after the hunting parties had left and the life of the village began to follow the usual pattern, he might be able to reach the medicine lodge unseen. He was lucky in that it was not the chief's, which was set in the middle of the circles of tepees, but apart on the northern edge. And perhaps, though he dreaded leaving the water, he could work his way around to it, using the tall grass for cover. If there was no one inside, he could get in easily enough, for the skin wall at the back would split under his teeth.

So, patiently, Yellow Shell lay in the water, only his head, under the shadow of a willow, above the surface of the stream, watching carefully all he could see of the camp.

Someone beat a drum with quick, sharp taps, and then a howling call rang out in a summons. He saw braves trotting towards the centre of the village to answer. Not a war party. There had been no dancing, no singing. No, he must have been right in his guess—a hunt was now intended. And by the numbers in the pack so assembled, the prey to be was no easily attacked beast. Could they be after the horned ones of the prairie? Yellow Shell gave a short snort at the thought. What powerful medicine *must* hang in their midst if these thought they could bring down a buffalo! Yet so large a gathering of hunters could not be aimed at any lesser game.

He saw a part of the pack as they trotted out. At the fore went a mighty coyote with lighter fur that showed almost white in the twilight where it was not dabbed with paint. He was flanked by the seasoned warriors of the village. Trailing this impressive van were younger hunters, some hardly out of cubhood, bringing up the rear. These did not prance or bark, but padded humbly in their elders' wake as if deeply impressed by the task now before them.

Yellow Shell waited until they were long gone, for they headed north into the grassland, thus verifying his suspicion that it was indeed buffalo they were going to run. And he wondered at the daring of the chief who had planned this hunt, which even the Wolf Tribe would think twice of attempting, old enemies of the horned ones that they were.

By the rise of the moon the camp was not quite so busy. Many of the cubs were down splashing in the river. Yellow

Shell had edged back into the grassland, his nose wrinkling when the smell of meat from the tepees reached him. As he went deeper into the prairie, he used his keen scent to find certain leaves, pleased when he came across a sage bush very aromatic in the night wind.

Now he smeared more of the crushed leaves well into his coat, along the scaly skin of his powerful tail. As a cover it might not be all he could wish, but the coyotes were so keen of nose that he needed all the protection he could find. The wind blew now from the east, which was a small thing in his favour. But he hated to travel on land, which was always hard for him.

Once again he scuttled from bush to bush, working around in a wide half circle that he might approach the camp from the north, and thus be closest to the medicine lodge. To get right against its back was his hope. He could listen at its wall, and if he heard no movement within, he would take a chance and slit the skin.

What he would do with the bag he sought once he had it in his paws. Yellow Shell did not yet know. The spirit dream had shown him that this he must do in order to help himself, and so he would follow its direction.

When the leaves were only green-grey smears on the pads of his paws, he gave a last wipe of those paws on his haunches and moved out. There was a stir in the village, but it did not reach the medicine lodge. Perhaps the coyotes had good reason to be in awe of the Changer, though all knew that he favoured the coyotes as brothers and wore their shape more often than any other, dwelling among them for periods of time, to their great joy.

Now and again Yellow Shell gave an anxious glance to the sky. He had not forgotten the crows he had seen flying in this direction, though in all his scouting of the village he had not seen them here. Perhaps they had brought some message, and, that task done, had left again.

With a last burst of the best speed a beaver could summon on land, Yellow Shell reached the position he had aimed for, right at the back of the medicine lodge. He edged as close as he could, laying his ear against its surface, trying to hold his breath and still a little the fast beating of his own heart, so that he could listen the better and catch any small sound from within.

The noises of the camp were annoying; he could not block them out well enough to be sure that there was not a sleeper inside. But after a long wait, the beaver knew that he could not remain there, doing nothing. He would have to make up his mind before the return of the hunting party. They must pass close to where he crouched and he had little hope that his smearing of sage and other scented leaves would cover him from their keen noses.

He began to dig a little with his forepaws, pausing fearfully after every scoop or two to listen. But there was no sound. At last his fear of being discovered by the hunters' return grew stronger than his caution, and he snapped at the skin wall of the tepee near the bottom where he had made a hollow in the earth. Three such slashing attacks and he had an opening large enough for his head and shoulders.

Immediately before him, tickling his nose and providing a screen, was a heaping of dried grass and sage twigs for a bed place. There was no fire in the circle of ash-smeared stones in the centre of the lodge. No one was there.

Yellow Shell wriggled all the way in, to sit up on the bed and look about. There were no food-storage bags or water carriers hanging from the poles set up against both sides of the lodge to support such, on the right and left of the front flap door. And under him the bedding was dusty dry, crunched as he moved, as did stuff long gathered that had not been lately put to use.

He could smell coyote, yes, but not as strongly as if one had recently lived here. And he began a wary circuit, using his nose to tell him what might have happened here.

The smell of dried meat clung faintly to the poles for the storage bags. And there was also the scent of herbs, which might be part of medicine. But he was not ready for the disappointment that awaited him as he straightened to his full height under the centre pole of the tepee and stretched back his head to see where the bundle had hung in the dream. There was nothing there.

Of course, the Changer would have taken the bag with him when he went. But where—where now must Yellow Shell follow or search? The beaver slumped to all fours, the pain of his sore feet, the aches in his body suddenly the sharper. And the misery of not knowing what to do next was a dark shadow over his mind.

As he so crouched closer to the beaten earth, he caught sight, very plain in the gloom of the lodge, of a small bit of white—a piece of eagle down. And he knew it for a thing of power. His dream—the bundle—it had been wrapped in a skin bag with tassels of fur and feathers dangling from it. This would seem to be a part of one such tassel. Carefully Yellow Shell picked it up between two claws.

The White Eagle! Not the mighty Storm Cloud of the heights, but a far greater chief than he. Because the White Eagle truly ruled the sky below the Sky Country, and only by his will might one pass safely from the world below to the world above. Forever did he sit on a far higher peak than any Storm Cloud knew, a peak in the north. Always he faced the sunrise, but on his right and to his left sat two younger eagles. And he on the right was the Speaker who faced north, and he on the south was the Overseer. Those flew at intervals high above the world so that they might see all that happened, reporting to the White Eagle how it fared with land, water, beasts and growing things.

So this white down was the sign of the White Eagle and a precious thing of much power. Holding it so, Yellow Shell knew a slight spurt of hope, knew what he could now try. So when he crawled out of the lodge, he took with him that wisp of feather.

Now—to find a high place. He hunched up to look about him. The river had rocks along its banks farther to the east. At the moment those were the highest spots the beaver could sight. There was no hope to return in time to the mountains, or even to the foothills. He had this to encourage him—a rising and a strong wind that now tugged at him.

In his haste to try out his plan for finding where the Changer had gone with the medicine bag, Yellow Shell almost lost his caution. It was only a series of sharp barks from the direction of the prairie that reminded him that he must still be alert to what lay there, to the hunters who might at any moment return. And it seemed that that was just what was happening now. For at that barking there were more echoes from among the lodges and he saw the squaws and older cubs gathering in excitement, the younger of them heading out, in his direction, as if to meet the returning warriors.

With a burst of speed difficult for his heavy body, Yellow Shell scuttled as fast as he could towards the river, putting such a screen of grass and brush between him and the village as he could find, hoping to reach the river to the east well beyond the village.

He was soon almost winded, for this was rough ground and his fear pushed him to greater and greater efforts. The barking chorus behind him took on the measure of a song and he thought he read triumph in it. The warriors of the camp might be back from a battle or successful raid— anyway, it was plain they had accomplished something of which they were proud.

Yellow Shell did not pause to look back, nor had he any eyes for anything but the ground immediately around him. If he could but reach the water—As it had been yesterday, the need for water was now like a whip laid across his haunches.

Here was a rise of rocks, those he had picked out as a good base for his try at using the eagle down. But he had no thought of that now; even in the night he could be sighted by those hunters from the plains. Instead he plunged into the first opening he saw between those rough stones, scrambling up and down, sometimes slipping painfully on pebbles and gravel caught in the hollows between them, until he came once more to a drop, with the stream lying below.

Taking the precious feather carefully into his mouth, Yellow Shell thankfully dived in, allowed the water to close over him, hardly daring to believe even now that he had managed to leave the village without raising an alarm. Could it be that the power of the spirit dream somehow clung to him, so that just as he had visited the lodge by dream undetected by the coyotes, so he was now also able to go in body?

He swam upstream, ready to duck beneath the surface of any pool if the need arose. The river-bed was narrower here, channelled between steadily rising banks of stones embedded in sun-hardened clay. He put as much distance between him and the camp as he could, alert to any sound from behind that would warn that he was being trailed.

But perhaps whatever success the hunters had had so satisfied the coyotes that they were aware of nothing else. Again he wondered if they had indeed brought down a buffalo, for to those whom the Changer favoured, such a coup might well be possible.

Dawn found him on much higher ground, the stream now running swiftly and with a force he found increasingly difficult to battle against. He pulled out of its grip at last. There were no alders, willows, or edible roots here, and he regretted not having brought supplies with him. But hunger could not turn him back now.

The feather plume, when he took it carefully out of his mouth, was almost as wet as if he had switched it through the river. He held it up with great care to where the breeze blew, trying to dry it. And as he did so, he chanted, though he did not raise his voice above the mutter of the water behind him:

"Eagle, hear me—
Let your power be with me.
White Eagle, hear me.
Speaker, hear me.
Overseer, the seeker, hear me.
White is this,
Of your medicine.
Let the wind that is the beating
Of your wings in the sky
Carry this, which is of your own power,
To join with that which is of its own.
Carry high, and carry far,
To join again that which is its own!"

He pulled from around his neck what was left of his neck-laces and looped them with one paw about the haft of his spear, for this was all he had to offer. Then he threw the spear and the dangling ornaments up into the sky with all the force left in his tired foreleg. It rose, swept on and on and was gone beyond the rocky wall. And Yellow Shell was heartened, for it had not tumbled back into the stones where he could see. But as long as he was able to watch, it had gone up and up. Perhaps White Eagle would be pleased to notice his offering, and would listen with an attentive ear to his singing.

Holding the feather still in the drying breeze with one forepaw, Yellow Shell scrambled up and up to follow the general direction of his vanished spear. It was not an easy climb and he was puffing hard through a half-open mouth as he reached the top.

Dawn was grey in the sky, the sun's day paint beginning to show on the eastern sky. The river had made a wide curve and now he could see that its source lay somewhere to the north, not the east, perhaps in the very mountains where Storm Cloud's tribe nested.

Once more the beaver chanted his petition to the White Eagle. And out of the river valley, or so it seemed, curled a breeze that although not forceful enough to be termed a wind, yet blew steadily.

Into this Yellow Shell loosed the feather. It was caught up in the breeze, to be borne southward into the desert waste on this side of the river. And with firm faith that he was indeed following a sure guide, the beaver set out after it.

It was light enough to see the feather clearly, to be able to follow its flight. So small a thing to trust to—For the first time in many hours, Cory thought as himself and not as Yellow Shell. Surely he could not depend upon such a thing as this!

But because the faith of his Yellow Shell self was so strong, Cory did not struggle against it.

To his surprise, it almost seemed that the feather *was* indeed a purposeful guide. Twice, Yellow Shell tired and crouched panting, unable to keep on. Then the feather was caught temporarily, to flutter on the top of some sun-dried, leafless piece of dead growth, only to be torn loose and carried on when the beaver was ready to shuffle ahead. Finally a last gust whirled it up and up into the bright blue of the cloudless sky as the beaver came to the edge of a basin.

This might be twin to that cupped-mountain stronghold of the eagles. But whereas that had been green and held water, this held sand, with strange, rough columns rising out of it, some of which had been toppled to lie full length.

Set up in the heart of this was a small skin shelter before which crouched an oddly shaped figure. It was busy, its forepaws patting and pulling at a mass of clay on the ground before it. Now and then it sprinkled water from a gourd on to that mass, always returning to its pinching and pulling, kneading and rolling.

The feather was like a snowflake, drifting through a winter day. As the beaver watched, it floated downward once more, heading straight for the worker. And Yellow Shell knew that he had found the Changer, though what he did here, the beaver could not guess.

Carefully he climbed down the basin wall, scurrying as fast as he could into the shadow of the nearest of those pillars, putting it between him and the Changer. As he set a paw on it, he found it was stone, yet once it must have been a tree, for it had the look of bark and wood. And if so, this must have been woodland changed to stone. Another trick of the Changer? If so, for what purpose? How could trees of stone serve anyone—Unless the Changer had been merely using his power for sport and to see what he might accomplish.

Yellow Shell crept on, though under his thick coat of fur he felt cold enough to shiver. The sun might be beating hotly down on his slowly moving body, yet the closer he drew to that absorbed worker, the more he felt a deep chill of fear.

Perhaps the Changer would catch sight of the eagle down, know that it had guided someone to spy on him. And what would be the fate of such a spy? To be changed—perhaps to such stone as these trees? Go back, said his fear. Yet Yellow Shell shuffled on, from one patch of shadow to the next.

He could hear the faint murmur of song now, and he guessed that the worker strove to sing into his fashioning of the clay some power. Yet it would seem that he was not accomplishing what he wished. For time and time again he would bring the full weight of his forepaws down on the clay, smashing it all flat again, growling over the destruction of his efforts.

Forepaws? Yellow Shell blinked (Cory would have exclaimed aloud had he then his human lips and voice). Those paws had looked like yellow coyote paws from a distance. But now—now they seemed to be human fingers busy once again at pushing, pinching, rolling—

He saw that the squatting figure was neither wholly an animal nor a man, but a strange combination of the two, as if someone had started to make a change from beast to man and the experiment had been only half successful.

Hands were at the end of furred forelegs, and the head was domed, as a human skull, though large ears pricked on either side. It was as if a man wore a beast's mask over his whole head. The hind legs were still pawed, but the shoulders under the yellow-brown hide were those of a man.

To Cory-Yellow Shell the combination was worse than if one wholly coyote or wholly human had been squatting there. To Cory the beast-human was all wrong and to be feared, while his Yellow Shell self found the human-beast unnatural and frightening. Yet the beaver could no longer retreat; he was held where he was as if bound to the column behind which he hid. And that realization came with such a shock that he whimpered aloud.

The singer's head lifted, green beast's eyes looked straight at the stone tree behind which Yellow Shell crouched. The Changer made a swift gesture, a beckoning. Against his will the beaver's body obeyed that summons, creeping out into the sun, treading straight to where the Changer worked in clay, with no hope of escaping that powerful pull.

About the Changer was a wide patch of dug-up earth, pocked with holes out of which he must have scraped his clay. A big mass of it was directly before him, having no form at all now, for he had just once more pounded what he shaped into nothingness. He sat, his man's hands resting upon its surface, watching the beaver. And he no longer sang, but rather he studied, as if he saw a use in Yellow Shell, as if some missing part to what he would shape had come to him.

Seeing that look, the beaver's terror grew, and with it an inner stir in his human self also. Cory must now break through this nightmare, awake into the real world before something worse happened. He could not guess what that something was, but the beaver's fear was a warning and he knew it too—as great as the terror that had touched him when he had watched the buffalo and the dancer.

A Shaping of Shapes

"What have we here?" The Changer spoke, and it seemed to Yellow Shell that his words were beaver, but to Cory's ears they were human. "You have come here to take the wood-which-is-stone for the making of spear points?" He nodded to one of the fallen pillars where its side had been chipped and broken, shattered lumps lying in the sand. "But, no, I think you have come for another reason, and it is one that can well serve my purpose. Now sit you and watch!"

And with those words he seemed to root Yellow Shell to the ground, for the beaver could not move, nor was he able to turn his eyes from the Changer's hands.

Once more the Changer mixed a little water from the gourd into the pile of moist clay, and his fingers pushed and pulled at the stuff. What arose from the muddy mixture under his coaxing was a small figure that very roughly resembled a man. There were two legs, two arms, a squat body, and a round blob ball for a head. But it was very crude, and plainly its maker was dissatisfied, for with his fist he impatiently smashed it back into the clay once more.

Cory came fully to life in the beaver body, aroused to take control at the sight of the manikin that had so disappointed its maker. And he spoke, though the sounds he made were a beaver's gutturals.

"You are making a man!"

The Changer stopped kneading the clay, his head swung up so those green eyes stared at Cory, or the beaver Cory now was. Very cold, very frightening were those eyes. Yellow Shell, the beaver, might not have been able to meet that stare for long, but Cory, the boy, somehow found courage and held steady. Slowly that gaze changed from cruel menace to surprise, and then speculation.

"So—you are that one," the Changer said.

What he meant by that, Cory did not know. But he continued to face the half man, half coyote with all the will he could summon to his aid. And now he had an idea. He did not know how such a thought had come, but he grasped it with a new boldness, as if to beaver stubbornness he added what only a human could know. He did not reply to the Changer's half question, but he said:

"You are trying to make a man."

Once more those green eyes were chill with anger—Cory did not know whether it was his guess or the Changer's own failure. A mud-spattered hand half rose as if to aim a blow at the beaver. Then it fell back on the clay, which he began to pinch and twist again in moist chunks, though now his attention was more on Cory than on what he was trying to do.

"You would bargain—with *me?*" There was a challenge in that demand.

"I offer you a model," Cory returned and waited in suspense, but with some hope. Would the Changer accept, turn him back to his human self for the sake of a model to copy for his manikin?

And if he were once more a boy, could he stay that way? Could he find his way back to his own world and time? The medicine bundle was what he needed to bargain with the Changer—Raven and the spirit dream had made that plain. And the medicine bundle was gone from the lodge in the coyote village. The Changer was working, or trying to work, strong magic here, so he must need that powerful bundle. As yet Cory had had no chance to look around, but perhaps if he got the Changer to believe he would be willing to aid in this present task, he could be given that chance.

The Changer's fingers were still now. He began to wipe the mud from them by scraping one hand over the other, until they were clean of most of the moist mass. All the time he eyed Cory as if he were measuring, weighing, turning the beaver inside out to get at what might lie beneath his furry hide.

Would he get out the bundle? Did he need to bring it into the open if he were to make Cory human once more? But the Changer was apparently in no hurry. He still rubbed his hands together, but absently now, as if his thoughts were very busy elsewhere.

Then he began to sing, a low-voiced chant. Cory could not understand the words, but the beaver's body began to shiver, chills ran along his spine, down forelimbs and back legs. The broad, powerful tail twitched, rose a little to beat up and down, hitting the ground in a thumping he could not control. The bond that had tied Yellow Shell in place no longer held.

Instead the beaver began to dance, against his will. He moved to no familiar beat of drum or ankle rattle, no sounding of turtle shell filled with pebbles, but to the song the Changer sang. Faster and faster he danced, whirling about in a dizzying circle that made his head spin so that he felt he could no longer see, or think, or breathe.

On and on he spun in that bewildering circle until there was nothing left in the world but that singing, loud as the crackle of lightning, the roll of storm thunder across mountain tops. Still Yellow Shell danced.

As suddenly as he had begun, the singer stopped. Once more Yellow Shell—no, not the beaver but the boy Cory—stood foot-rooted to the ground directly before the pile of mud from which the Changer was trying to shape his man. But Cory no longer wore Yellow Shell's thick fur, his paws, his tail. In so much had he won—he was a boy again.

However, he could not move, as he speedily discovered. He was as much a prisoner standing here as he had been when tied by the mink ropes. And now fear returned to him as he saw the animal jaws of the Changer open in a knowing grin, as if the other could read his thoughts and took pleasure in defeating his hopes. Perhaps—Cory shivered in spite of the sun's heat on his head and shoulders—perhaps this strange creature could do just that.

Still keeping his green eyes on Cory, the Changer began to work again with the clay, pinching, prodding, pulling it into shape, not looking at what he was doing at all, but rather at the boy's body. But it would seem that this method worked, for the manikin that now grew under his fingers was no rough figure but far more of a human shape. And he sang as he worked, words that Cory did not understand, though he recognized quickly that it was a song of power.

Up and up rose the figure the Changer made. Now it was as tall as Cory's knees, as his waist, and still it grew as the Changer's hands moved faster and faster, his singing grew louder. Never did he look at what he fashioned, but always at the boy, though once or twice he leaned over to spit into the mud, and again he threw into the clay pinches of some dusty stuff he took from a small pouch belted around his misshapen, half-beast body.

Now the manikin stood as tall as Cory's shoulder. As yet the head remained only a ball, but the body was clearly done. And Cory's fear deepened, for there was this about the Changer's work—as it grew more human, so did Cory hate it more. It was as though it might be a great enemy, or the sum of all his own fears from both worlds.

The Changer dropped his hands and for the first time his eyes left Cory, so the boy felt a sense of relief, as if that intent stare had held him prisoner. Now the shaper looked from Cory to the image of mud and back again with long measurement, though the ball head of the figure remained unfinished.

Apparently satisfied with his work, the Changer edged backward without rising to his feet, putting his hands to the ground on either side to pull himself along. Again Cory felt relief from some loosening of the will that held him. But he guessed that it was best not to betray he had that small freedom, lest the Changer turn his full attention once more on his prisoner.

Now the Changer pulled sticks before him, so that they

lay between him and the image he had created. He set these up for a fire as the otters had their signal, in the form of a te-pee. But he did not touch light to it at once. Instead he took from his belt pouch some small packets of leaves folded in upon themselves, each fastened with sharp thorns into tight packages. These he unpinned one by one, to display small amounts of what might be dried herbs or dust.

Cory was deeply afraid now, though as yet he had not been openly threatened. If he could have done so he would have run, just as he had from the buffalo and the dancer. But, though he was somewhat freed from the bonds the Changer had so mysteriously laid upon him, he was not free enough to leave. He knew, he could not tell how—unless that was part of Yellow Shell's beaver memory still lingering with him—that if he could not fight now, it would be the end of him. For the Changer's full medicine would be too strong for him to withstand.

Too strong for animals—but what about man? How had that thought come to Cory? Animal—man. Man *was* an animal, but also more, sometimes only a little, but still more. Thoughts raced in his mind. If he let the Changer complete the magic he would do here—then perhaps man would never be that little bit more, though he could not tell how he knew that.

Suddenly, as clearly as if his eyes actually saw it before him—a picture formed in his mind—the head of a black bird. Crow—such as served the Changer? No! There were white circles about the eyes and the bird's beak opened to voice a medicine song—Raven!

And it seemed to Cory that when he thought the name

Raven, the picture in his mind turned its eyes on him and a new picture formed, by the will and power of Raven. Another bird head—this one white—Storm Cloud? No, it was a greater eagle. And he remembered the White Eagle to whom Yellow Shell had appealed when he loosed the bit of down that had guided him here.

But what had the White Eagle to do with—? Again as he identified the picture, that majestic bird also turned to look squarely at him and once more came another picture. But this one was vast, clouded, he could see only a bit of it, and he sensed with awe that it was given to no one to see the whole of what stood there.

And perhaps it was the remnants of Yellow Shell's memory that gave an awesome name to that half-seen shadow. For that it was awesome even the human Cory recognized. Thunderbird! And when he named it in his mind it became clearer for a single instant. But Cory could never afterwards recall just what he had seen then, or if he had seen anything at all, but had only been blinded by the appearance of something it was not given to his kind to understand.

But Thunderbird's shadow remained with him. And to that vague picture Yellow Shell's memory added some words that were strong medicine—very strong. Cory did not repeat them aloud, but he turned his head to look at the mud image, which moment by moment grew less and less like clay, more and more like brown skin laid over firm flesh, upheld by solid bone.

Cory studied the ball of a head that had never been truly finished, and in his mind he repeated the medicine words, trying to shut out all but those words and the need for saying them over and over. Why it was necessary to do this he could not say, only that it was all he *could* do to prevent the Changer from completing his purpose.

Smoke with a strong smell puffed up around him, but drifted more towards the image, clinging to the mud. Then hands reached out to grasp the clay body on either side of its slender waist, lifted it up. Cory, still watching, repeated the words in his mind now with all his energy. He saw the Changer set the mud man down with its feet in the blazing, smoking fire, so that the flames rose up about it.

Then the Changer stood up, his half-man, half-beast form even stranger looking when he was erect. And he began a medicine song. But Cory tried to shut his ears to the sound, to think only of the words that would call the Thunderbird. While his feet could not move from where they appeared to be fixed to the ground, he found he could raise his hands somewhat. And they moved now in signs following the words in his mind.

At first the flames rose very high, shoulder high around the image, and the smoke veiled it from view. There was a feeling of triumph, of success in that smoke, and in the singing.

Still Cory's hands moved to match the words in his mind and perhaps the Changer was so intent upon his own magic that he did not see what Cory did.

Then the smoke rippled and a wind rose out of nowhere. The sun was clouded and a chill edged the breeze. The dance and song pattern of the Changer altered. He took a step or two more, then stood, looking about him with quick wariness, as if he had been shocked out of a dream.

The wind not only whipped away the smoke but it pulled at the live brands of the fire, whirling one up in a shower of sparks, carrying it away, to be followed by a second, a third. The Changer cried out, but his voice sounded more like the howl of a coyote. He flung up his hand as if to stop one of those flying torches, and the fire of it must have singed him painfully, for again he howled in rage.

His eyes flamed yellow-green, turning from the wind-driven fire to Cory, and his lips drew back to show the fangs of a hunting beast. He vigorously made signs with his man hands. For a moment the wind died a little, the showering sparks did not fill the air.

Only now the clouds had so darkened the sky that they made a low ceiling. Cory felt that if he reached up his arm he could touch them. From those clouds broke flashes of lightning and the Changer whirled at the first brilliant crackling, as if he could not believe in this sudden storm.

He snarled at the flashes, again showing his fangs, and voiced a long, wailing howl. He might have been ordering those clouds to clear, the sun to shine again. But only for a moment he stood so, looking up into the gathering fury. Then he turned, his anger visible in every upstanding hair on his shoulders, in the prick of his ears, the wrinkling of his lips.

Once more his hands moved in signs. The bit of Yellow Shell still in Cory cringed at the sight of those. For, not being a medicine beaver, he could not read the signs, yet in them he saw great power.

Cory's thoughts faltered; he could no longer remember clearly those words that had spoiled what the Changer meant to do here. But his failure to keep up the fight did not seem to matter. Perhaps he had only prepared the way for another force that would now take over, whether he continued to call it or not.

His hands fell heavily to his sides, as if once more chained there. And he could not move, even when one of the wind-blown brands burned his neck with its sparks, singeing his hair.

For if the wind had subsided a little at the Changer's retort, it rose again, scattering the fire as if a broom had been used for that purpose. And the flames were almost gone as huge drops of rain fell with the force of blows on the ground, on the dying coals, on the mud image, and on Cory.

Now the Changer stood to his full height, his Coyote head flung back on his man's shoulders, his eyes searching the sky as he turned his head slowly. It was as if he looked to find his enemy above, searched there for a target against which to loose his powers.

For a long moment he stood so, while the coals of fire hissed black and dead under the pelting of the rain and it grew colder and colder. Cory, who only moments earlier had felt the terrible heat of the sun in this desert place, now shivered and shook under the blast of the chill.

Seeming at last to have made up his mind, the Changer turned his back on the now dead fire, on the image standing in what had been its heart. He went to one of the dead bushes nearby and, stooping down, laced the fingers of his right hand among its branches, bringing it up out of the ground in a single pull.

Its roots made a tangle from among which he plucked a

bag. Cory, seeing it, knew that this was what Yellow Shell had hunted. This was the Changer's great medicine; with it in hand he was armed, ready to stand firm against all the spirits of sky, earth, water, and air.

With both hands he held it aloft, into the full force of the storm, shaking it from side to side as if it were a dance rattle, or as if he wanted the spirits in that punishing wind to be well aware of with what he threatened them.

The wind died, the rain ceased, the clouds began to split apart. All the while the Changer, holding high his mighty power, danced and sang. That singing was not for the ears of man, it was stronger than any lightning crackle, any cruel roll of thunder.

Still the Changer danced and sang, and held the medicine bundle as one might hold a spear against an enemy, driving away the storm that had spoiled all his plans. For how long he danced so, Cory could not have said, for time no longer had a meaning.

But at last even the Changer must have grown tired, for Cory could see again, hear again. And the beast-man sat upon the ground even as he had when first Yellow Shell had looked down into the forest of stone trees. There was now only a shapeless mass of clay where the image had stood, flowing down from a blob supported on two legs that the fire had baked into a more enduring substance.

The Changer lifted the hand holding the medicine bundle and tapped that mass lightly, and straightway even the legs became mud again. He looked down for a long time at that sticky pile. Then he roused, threw back his head, and gave one of those far-sounding howls. Having done so, he stared at

Cory and there was such an evil glint in his narrow beast eyes that the boy tried vainly to fight the bonds laid upon him.

For a time the Changer made no move, though now and then he turned his head with the coyote ears a-prick as if he were listening. The sun went down, to leave them in the night. No fire burned and Cory's human sight could not pierce the darkness as Yellow Shell's had done. But, almost as if he wanted to prove to Cory that he had won, the Changer rebuilt the fire, though it was not in the same place as the other and he did not toss into it the contents of leaf packets.

There came a fluttering out of the dark, and feathered shapes lit on the ground, hopped into the circle of light about the fire. Crows—ten—twenty—more—coming and going so that Cory could not count them, or even be sure that they were not the same ones over and over. As each hopped past the Changer, he spat out on the ground a mouthful of yellow-brown clay, which the beast-man mixed with the other mass. And that grew taller and taller. Now he scraped and mixed it well, working the new and old clay together as he sang in a voice hardly louder than a murmur, as if he feared being overheard.

Some of the crows settled down on the other side of the fire. Cory noted that they showed interest, not in what their master was doing but in the medicine bag that lay close to him, for he had not returned it to hiding after using it to drive off the storm. And the boy knew that if he could but get it out of the Changer's reach, he could put an end to all that was happening here. But he could see no chance of that.

Knead, pinch, pull, shape—the Changer's human hands

moved faster, with a greater sureness than they had before, as if, having once made the manikin, his fingers remembered their task. But this time the figure he wrought was larger, was as tall in fact as a man, as Uncle Jasper.

Uncle Jasper. Cory blinked. That other world seemed so far away, so lost to him now. Yet, when he had thought of Uncle Jasper—Yes! His hands had been able to move: Uncle Jasper, the ranch—Dad—Just as he had seen the Raven, White Eagle, and that shadowy other in his mind, so now he tried to picture all he could that was most important to him of his own world and time. But, as he felt his bonds loosen, he did not try yet to move. Patience he had learned from Yellow Shell, and the determination to fight for survival, but some of this stubborn will to face danger was now Cory's own, either newborn or simply newly roused from a spark that had always been there, but that he had not known he had.

Let the Changer become so interested in his "man" that he would forget Cory. Even now he seldom looked at the boy; he appeared no longer to need him as a pattern.

And the birds—They had eyes only for the medicine bag. To reach it Cory would have to half circle the fire, but in a second, before he got so far, the Changer could snatch it to safety. His only hope was to wait for some chance.

Again the body stood finished, the head remaining a round ball. But this time the Changer went to work on that. He made no attempt to give it a human face. Instead the clay moved under his fingers into the shape of a long narrow jaw and nose, pointed ears—the head of a coyote, twin to the one on the Changer's own shoulders. He stood back at last to study it critically. Then, with finger-tips, went to work again, modifying the beast look somewhat. Still it was far more an animal's mask than any face. But that apparently was the result the Changer wanted.

Now for the first time in hours he looked directly at Cory with a tooth-showing grin.

"How like you my man?" he barked.

"It is not a man." Cory told him the truth.

"But it is the new man," the Changer told him. "For this is a man as he should be for the good of the People. And for the good of the Changer." Again he laughed, though it was more of a yapping.

"Yes," he continued, "this is man as the People need him, for to us he shall be a slave and not a master. These—" he touched the dangling mud hands almost contemptuously, "shall serve the People as sometimes paws cannot. These—" now he rapped the wide mud shoulders, then stooped to run a finger-tip down the clay legs, "shall bear burdens, run to our command. This is man as the Changer has made him, shaped from the earth, hardened, as he soon will be, by fire, made ready for the life—" now he turned to look at Cory with those evil, narrow eyes, "you shall give him!"

Cory cried out; he thought he screamed. And in that moment he was answered out of the dark, out of the sky—with a shriek that set the very earth trembling under them.

The Changer Challenged

Once more the sky was torn by broad purple flashes of lightning and a chill wind blew about them. In a half crouch, snarling, the Changer turned to face the dark beyond the fire.

Something moved there. Cory could not see it plainly; the clouds were so thick, the night so very dark. But he thought that great wings fanned, that a head as large as his own body turned so that burning eyes might look upon them. And the boy wanted to throw himself to the ground, dig into the sand, as if he were Yellow Shell diving into the river water.

The crows cried out, but they did not take to the air. Instead they cowered close to the ground, as if seeking shelter where there was no cover left. But the Changer now stood tall, his back to the fire and to his man of mud, facing the fluttering in the night.

"Hear me." He spoke as he would to Cory, yet even above the noise made by the crows, the drumming of the thunder, he could be heard. "I am He Who Shapes, and this is my power. You cannot deny it to me for it is mine!"

And he spoke as if he knew very well who or what was in the dark there, and felt confident that he could safely face it so.

Who—or what— This was the shadow that had risen behind the White Eagle in Yellow Shell's vision—this was the *Thunderbird!*

To Cory, Yellow Shell's memory supplied the rest—this was the Thunderbird whose presence was in the storm, the wind, the lightning, the pound of thunder, the rise of wind. The Thunderbird spoke for one being only—the Great Spirit.

"I am He Who Shapes, who changes," the Changer repeated, still confident, but faintly angry now. "This is my power and I hold it against all the spirit ones, great or small!"

The crows cawed together harshly. Then, instead of taking to wing, they scuttled out of the circle of light, taking shelter in the shadow of one of the trees lying prone. If they could dig their way into the sand, thought Cory, seeing their flight, they would be doing that right now.

There was a fanning of wings, so huge they could be felt as a rippling of the air, and after that a new crackling of lightning. But as yet no rain had appeared.

"Elder Brother, listen. We have no quarrel, no spear, no claw or fang now bared to make a red road running between us. You lead the storm clouds into battle, as was given you to do. I but do as was given me, I shape and change, shape and change. And now it is in me to shape one who will serve the People, who will not say 'Do this, do that,' 'Come be my meat and let me eat,' 'Come be my robe and let me wear.' For if I do not breathe life into this one, there shall come another somewhat like him but of another shaping, and then it shall be ill for the People, and all their greatness shall be gone. They will dwindle into less and less, and some shall vanish from mother earth, never to be seen again. I, the Changer, have foreseen this evil thing. And because I *am* the Changer, it is laid upon me to see that it will not come to be so."

"The time is not due, the shape is not right. It is not for you, Younger Brother, to do this, which is a great, great thing that none but the ONE ABOVE may do." The words rolled out of the dark with the beat of thunder, as if they were a chant sung to a drum.

"I am the Changer, Elder Brother. So was the power given me in the First Days, so it has always been. Such power once given cannot be taken away. That is the Right and the Law."

"That is the Right and the Law," agreed the voice from the dark. "But also it is the Right and the Law that one may challenge you, is that not also the truth?"

The Changer laughed in a sharp, yelping sound. "That's the truth, Elder Brother. But who can do so? For mine alone of the earth spirits is the shaping power. You, Elder Brother, can control the wind, the clouds, the lightning and thunder, the pound of rain, the coming of cold moons' snow. But can you shape anything?"

"The power is yours only—on earth," again agreed the shadow.

"And it is on earth now that we stand, Elder Brother. Therefore, I say that this shall be done—that I shall shape this 'man' to be a servant to the People. Nor will you again raise a storm to stop me, for when I have so spoken, then it becomes my right."

"It becomes your right," again echoed that mighty voice. "But still you may be challenged—"

"Not on my making of this thing," returned the Changer quickly.

"Then otherwise," replied the Thunderbird. "For it is this message that I bring—there shall be a challenge, and, if you lose, then you shall with your own hands destroy this thing you have shaped, and you shall forget its making and not so shape again. Instead you shall be guided for a space by the will and wishes of he who challenges."

"And if I win?" There was such confidence in the Changer that he seemed to be growing taller, larger, to match the shadowy giant Cory could more sense than see.

"And if you win, then it shall be as you have said. Though this thing is wrong, yet it shall live and be all you have promised, a servant to the People, never more than that."

"So be it! Such a tossing of game sticks pleases me. But since I am the challenged, I say that this testing shall be rooted in mother earth, for I am *her* son and not one who commands air, wind, and water as my right."

"So be it," agreed the Thunderbird in turn. "You have the choice that this contest be of the earth. Mine is the second saying, which is this—"

There was movement in the night as if mighty wings were spread, and Cory felt those eyes burning not only on the Changer and the image of mud but on him also. And in that moment he guessed that soon, if ever, would come his chance, and he must be ready to seize it. That binding the Changer had laid upon him still held in part, but suppose the Changer would be so occupied with this contest that he must use all his power for it? Then Cory would be wholly free. He could see the medicine bag still lying beside the fire, very plain in the light.

The Thunderbird had paused for a long moment, as if he were turning over in his mind several different possibilities of a challenge. At last he spoke.

"Of the earth, yet in a manner of seeing of my sky also. Look you to the north, Younger Brother. What see you?"

There was a vivid flash of lightning to tear aside the night, holding steady as no lightning Cory had ever witnessed before had done. Against it stood the black outline of a mountain, one of lesser width but greater height than the eagles' hold.

"I see earth shaped as a spearhead aimed at the sky," replied the Changer. "This is a piece of medicine to be thought on, Elder Brother. Perhaps it does not promise good for you."

"A piece of earth," answered the Thunderbird. "As you have asked for, Younger Brother. Now this be my challenge—which is not really mine but that of One Above speaking through me—that you take this earthen spear and without changing its form you lay it upon the ground so that it no longer aims its point to the sky, but into this desert country, even at this fire where you would harden your shaping into life."

Still that lightning banked behind the mountain, showing

it plainly. And the Changer looked at it steadily, nor did he show that he thought the task impossible.

"It is of the earth," he said, "and so must obey me." And to Cory he sounded as confident as ever.

Facing the mountain, he uttered some sharp howls, as if the huge mound of earth and stone were alive but sleeping, and must be so awakened to listen to his orders. Then his feet began to stamp, heavier and heavier and heavier, as he put his full force into each planting of those coyote paws.

Stamp, stamp, right paw, left paw—

Under his own feet Cory felt an answering quiver in the earth, as if the force of that stamping ran out under the surface.

Stamp, stamp—those paws were now digging holes into the ground where the Changer brought them down with all his might. At the same time he began to sing, pointing his human hands at the mountain peak against that light which could no longer be considered lightning, for it remained steady and clear.

And having pointed out the mountain, the Changer now went through the motions of hurling at the peak, although his hands held nothing Cory could see.

Stamp, hurl, stamp, hurl. Cory watched, yet the peak remained unchanged. And the boy wondered if there was any time limit placed upon this contest.

With a great effort he dragged his eyes away from the Changer and looked to where the medicine bundle lay. Now he began to try his strength once more against the spell the Changer had held him in. His hands moved to answer his will, and then his arms, stiffly, with pain, as if they had been cramped in one position too long. He tried not to flinch lest the Changer notice him. But the coyote head remained steadily facing the mountain.

Cory glanced up to see that the hurling motions had come to an end. Now the Changer moved right hand and arm in a wide, sweeping, beckoning. It might be that in answer to his signal he expected that distant humping of earth to take to itself legs or wings and come forward at his gesture.

If he expected such, he was doomed to disappointment. But Cory gave only a short glance at what the Changer did. He was edging, hardly more than an inch at a time, out of the place where he had been rooted for so long at the other's pleasure. Now the image stood between him and the Changer, and he had yet some feet to go around the fire to get his hands on the medicine bag. So much depended upon whether the Changer would remember him, or whether he would need the bag for his present magic. Cory could only try, for he believed that he would not get a second chance.

He stooped a little to flex his stiff knees, then stood erect several times, remaining still when it seemed that prick-eared head was about to turn. The crows had left off cawing, almost as if they feared they were distracting their master's attention at this great testing of his power. But they watched from where they were and perhaps they would betray Cory.

And what of that great shape? Had it indeed come to his call that first time when the storm had destroyed both the fire and the image baking in it? Yet Cory was sure, though he could not have said how he knew, that that shape was not really concerned with him at all, but only with what might happen when the Changer shaped his mud and thought of giving it life.

So Cory kept to his own purpose, to reach the medicine bag. With his hands on that, could he indeed escape the Changer's spells—return himself to his own world and time?

Still the Changer sang his song, beckoned to the mountain. Then, from far away, there was a rushing that became a roar and Cory, startled, looked round.

Where the mountain had stood stark and clear, shown only by the light the Thunderbird had summoned, now shot a red column of fire. A volcano?

And that fire climbed into the sky, as might a fountain. As the spray of a fountain falls, so did a shower of giant sparks come, together with brilliant streams channelling the earth of the peak's sides. The peak was being consumed. As its sides melted, so clouds gathered above it, dark and heavy. From them poured streams of rain, so that steam arose. And underneath him, as far from the mountain as he was, Cory could feel the ground weave and shake, move as if some great explosion tore under its surface.

Cory was thrown forward, his hands out, and the fire the Changer had built was scattered in brands that glowed and sputtered. Even the Changer was down on his hands and knees, and now he looked more animal than man. He was snarling, snapping at a flaming bit of wood that had seared against his upper arm.

The image he had made tottered back and forth, though it did not fall. And the Changer, seeing it in danger, made a sudden leap to steady it, brace it up against the continued shaking of the ground.

At the mountain the flames tore up and across the sky as if more than just one peak was now burning, or as if earth itself, and rock, could burn as easily as dried wood. But the flood from the sky poured steadily on it, drowning that fire bit by bit. Though they were miles away, they could hear the noise of that mighty battle between fire and water.

Under Cory's hand as he pushed against the ground to gain his feet was a smooth object. The medicine bag! He had the medicine bag! But where could he go—what could he do with it? He had no doubt the Changer could get it away from him with ease if he remained nearby.

A glance told him that the Changer was still occupied with saving his clay figure from breaking. Whether or not he could claim any victory in the contest, Cory did not know. The Changer was lowering the mountain, but not as the Thunderbird had directed—moving the point undisturbed out to lie pointing into the waste. And the storm the Thunderbird had summoned was putting an end to the fire.

Cory held the bundle tight against his chest. Then he scrambled to his feet and began to run, without any goal, just out into the desert, towards the wall of the basin that held the wood of stone. If the crows gave warning of his going, he did not hear them, for that roaring in the earth, in the sky, was a harsh sound filling the whole night.

Panting, he somehow got up the ridge, pausing there for a moment to look back. The fire had caught the small hide shelter of the Changer. From this point Cory could not see the shadowy form of the Thunderbird, only the beast-man steadying his image against one of the stone trees. Around and around above flew a wheeling circle of crows. And seeing that, Cory began to run again.

When he had first picked up the medicine bag, it had

seemed very light, as if it were stuffed only with feathers. But as he went it grew heavier and heavier, weighing against him so that at last he was drawn towards the earth. And he ran as if a prisoner's chain were fastened to his feet; his flight became a trot, and finally a walk. Now he was in the dark, though from behind, the glow of the melting mountain was like a sun rising, only in the north instead of the east. It sent his own shadow moving before him—and that shadow changed.

It had been a boy's as he left the hollow. Now it grew hunched of back, thicker—Cory looked down at his own body. There was fur, there were the webbed hind feet, the clawed forepaws, behind him a scaled tail dragged on the ground. His pace was the shuffle of a beaver. He was Yellow Shell again!

The heart almost went out of Cory. He had been sure he had won back his own body, if not his own world—but now—Now he had the medicine bag, yes, but he had lost himself again. And in a clumsy beaver body, in this desert place, he would have so little chance to escape—for this was coyote land and he did not doubt that the Changer would have the advantage.

Yet he continued to shuffle on, the heavy bag clasped tight to his chest with one forepaw while he walked on the other three with what speed he could make. Water—if he could only reach water! But this was desert. There was no water here.

Unless—unless the storm would have given some to the land, even if only for a short time before the sand drank it up!

Yellow Shell's sense, his quivering nose in a head thrown

as far back on his bulky shoulders as he could raise it, sought water. And the scent of it came to him—south and west. Unhesitatingly he turned to find that water.

He humped along at the best speed his beaver body was capable of making. And the bag grew ever heavier, chained and slowed him more and more. Yet he did not put it down, even for a breath of rest. He had a feeling that were he once to let it out of his hold, he would not be able to pick it up again.

The false sun of the blazing mountain was dying now. Perhaps the storm the Thunderbird had raised to quell the flames was winning. So his path grew darker. He now entered a world of sand dunes. To climb up and down carrying the weight of the bag was more than Yellow Shell dared attempt. He had a vision of being buried in some slip of a treacherous surface. So he had to turn and twist, push along such low places as he could find. As Cory he would have had no guide and might have become hopelessly lost. But as Yellow Shell the scent of water found him a path.

There came a cawing overhead. He did not have to look up to know that one of the crows must have sighted him, that even if the Changer had lost him for a time, now he was trailed again. That the beast-man would be after him at once, Yellow Shell did not doubt. His only hope was based on the fact that the scent of water was now stronger and that the dunes among which he slipped and slid were growing smaller and farther apart.

He came around a last one, was out on a stretch of rocky ground, great masses of it towering into the sky. The cawing over his head echoed and re-echoed. More of the crows joined in a flock. He expected them to attack him, to try to force him to drop the bag that now weighed upon him as if he had his foreleg around a big stone. But they only circled in the sky and called to their master.

With a last burst of the best speed he could make, Yellow Shell stumped across the stony land and came upon what he sought, a cut in the earth with the silver of water running through it. Though it was no true river, yet now it had a current that whirled along pieces of uprooted sagebrush and the long-dried remnants of other storms, so that to plunge blindly in with the weight of the bag was a dangerous thing. But not as dangerous, the beaver thought, as to remain on land where he was so clumsy and slow.

Without stopping to think or look behind, Yellow Shell dived, and the bag pulled him down and down, as if it would pin him to the bottom of the cut, hold him anchored so that the rush of the water, the beating of those floating pieces in it, would drown or batter him to death.

Yet Yellow Shell held to his stolen trophy, swimming along with the current with what strength he had, dragging the bag with him. It caught on rocks embedded in the bottom, on pieces of the drift, and he fought it almost as if it were a live enemy determined to finish him. But never did he loosen his hold upon it.

Then he was caught in a sudden eddy of the current. The bag loosened in his grip, almost whirled away. He fought to retain it but had to crawl half out of the water to do that. And at that moment he heard a noise that froze him where he was.

The howl of a coyote sounded so loud and sharp it seemed

as if the hot breath of that hunter were able to dry the fur rising in a fighting ridge on the beaver's back. Baring his mur-
derous teeth, Yellow Shell turned in the mud, tucking the bag
under his body, Cory's determination strengthening the animal stubbornness at facing old enemies.

Across the water was the Changer. But he himself had
changed. There was nothing of man left in the great yellow-
white beast who stood there. It was all animal, and the yellow eyes, the teeth from which the snarling lips curled away,
promised only death.

Yellow Shell snarled back. His forepaws were set tightly
on the medicine bag, and now he lowered his head, nipping
the taut surface of the bundle with his teeth, his intent plain.
Let the Changer move at him and he would destroy what he
had taken.

The coyote watched him. As the fire on the mountain had
paled, so now the first streaks of dawn lighted the sky. And
once more in Yellow Shell's mind came a faint and ghostly
vision of Raven, behind him the White Eagle, and farther
yet—the Thunderbird. Somehow, from them, added knowledge came to his aid.

Hold—if he could hold here and now until the sun rose.
And then let the sunlight touch upon the bag, so would the
Changer's power be broken. For he had used much of it, too
much of it, upon the mountain, which had not answered his
call but been consumed in part. In this much he had lost the
battle, but he would try again—unless his medicine was also
destroyed.

Knowing this, Cory-Yellow Shell crouched low above the
bag, sheltered it with his body. None too soon, for if the

crows had held off attack before, they did not do so now, but flew down and against him, striking with punishing beaks at his head, his eyes, stabbing his body painfully, though the thickness of his fur was some armour. Using his tail to defend himself as best he could, Yellow Shell stayed where he was, covering the bag.

With the attack from the birds there came also a different attack, aimed not against his body but his mind. A strong will battled against him, sought to make him give up what he had stolen. First it promised what he wanted most, his own body, return to his own world. Yet Cory-Yellow Shell did not yield. Then it threatened that he would never again be Cory, never return to the world he knew, while the crows dived and pecked at him until he was bleeding from countless small wounds on his head and shoulders.

The first red was in the sky, and that grew while the coyote prowled up and down the bank of the now fast-drying stream, and the crows cawed their hatred and rage overhead. Why the Changer did not attack in person, Cory did not understand. But the running water seemed to form a barrier he could not cross. Only the water was shrinking fast, and then—

It was a race between the coming of the sun and the vanishing of the water. If the water failed first, then Yellow Shell had no hope at all. Yet the beaver crouched and waited.

Sun—a first beam struck across the ground. Yellow Shell cried out as one of the crows struck viciously at his eye. He did not hesitate or try to protect himself, but used all his remaining strength to push the bundle out into that weak beam as it became stronger and stronger.

As if the sun had lighted a fire, smoke rose from the bundle, puffed out and out—

Cory coughed, coughed again, staggered back a step or two. He stood on two feet, he was a boy again. And in his hands he held the bundle—or was it the bundle? For it crumbled as might dried clay, sifting through his fingers in the fashion of fine sand. Then there were only particles of ashy dust left. The smoke blew away from him and he looked about as one just awakened from sleep.

Sleep—dream— He was at the line camp! There was the jeep, the corral, the horse and—Black Elk.

The old Indian sat with his blanket wrapped around his shoulders in spite of the heat. It was not dawn but late afternoon.

"What—what happened?" Cory's voice sounded small, frightened, and he was then ashamed of that sound.

"World turned over," Black Elk answered.

"The Changer—"

"He was." Black Elk looked directly at Cory for a second. Was there, or was there not (for a moment Cory felt the old chill of fear) a yellow glint in those eyes? If it served as a reminder of the Changer himself, it was gone in an instant.

"He was, he will be," Black Elk spoke. "Medicine things, they are not for the white man."

"No." Cory was eager to agree. He wiped his hands vigorously against his jeans, trying to smear off the last of the clinging dust that had been the bag.

"World turn over again," Black Elk continued. "Time coming—"

"It was a dream." Cory backed away from the fire and the old Indian. "Just a dream."

"Dreams spirit things, sometimes true," Black Elk said. "Indian learns from dreams—white man laughs, but Indian knows. You not laugh now, I think."

"No," Cory agreed. He certainly did not feel like laughing. He glanced at that safe anchor to the real world, the jeep. But now, somehow he had no need for such an anchor. The horse whinnied and Black Elk spoke again.

"Horse wants drink. You take—down to river—now!"

Cory moved without hesitation to obey the order. He laid his hand without shrinking on the curve of the Appaloosa's neck and the horse blew at him, snorted. But Cory felt light and free inside, and knew that he had lost the tight burden of his fear. No—he did not need the jeep as an island of safety in a world that had been so strange and dark and threatening, but was now more like an open door to the learning of many things.

He led out the Appaloosa. When he passed Black Elk, the old Indian's eyes were closed as if he slept.

The river was where he had seen the buffalo and the masked dancer. Were those, too, part of the dream, of the world that had not yet turned over? He did not know, but with every step he took, Cory began to understand that what he had learned as Yellow Shell was now a never-to-be-forgotten part of Cory Alder.

Had the Changer (he could see him—the Raven, the Eagle, the misty shape which was the Thunderbird—now in his mind for an instant), had the Changer indeed really reshaped him? Not into a beaver, but into someone stronger than he had been before he had worn fur and stood in a stone forest daring to summon a power greater than himself?

The horse had raised his dripping muzzle from the water. Almost without thinking, Cory guided him to a fallen tree trunk, using that for a mounting block to scramble somewhat awkwardly but with determination into the saddle. He gathered up the braided leather thong of the Indian halter, and with growing confidence turned his mount's head by a steady pull.

He rode up the slope, his pride growing. And now he suddenly heard thundering hoofs, saw the running of some free colts, and behind, the dusty figures of three riders.

Fur Magic—he could not tell why it had been his. But he sat quietly in Black Elk's saddle to face Uncle Jasper, the western sun warm on him, feeling very much a part of a new world.

Fur Magic

BY ANDRE NORTON

ABOUT THIS GUIDE

The information, activities and discussion questions which follow are intended to enhance your reading of *Fur Magic*. Please feel free to adapt these materials to suit your needs and interests.

ABOUT THE AUTHOR

Alice Mary Norton was born in Cleveland, Ohio on February, 17, 1912. Perhaps because her mother began reading to her when she was very young, she grew up loving books and began writing in high school. She published her first book, *The Prince Commands*, at the age of twenty. Norton wrote under a pseudonym which she felt helped her gain footing in male-dominated publishing markets, legally changing her name to Andre Alice Norton in 1934. She worked as a librarian in the Cleveland Public Library system, briefly owned a bookstore, and served as a reader and anthologist for publisher Martin Greenburg before devoting herself exclusively to writing. Norton's work spans decades and literary genres—her list of books, stories and poems numbering into the hundreds—though she is best known for her fantasy and young adult novels, including the Witch World series. Her Magic books, including *Fur Magic,* were largely written during the Vietnam era and feature young outsiders struggling to fit in and make sense of their worlds through fantastical journeys to times past. Norton received numerous accolades, including the Nebula Grand Master Award (1984), the Daedalus Award for Lifetime Achievement (1986), and the World Fantasy Convention Life Achievement

Award (1998). During the year 1997, "The Lady" as she was known to her myriad fans was inducted into the Science Fiction and Fantasy Hall of Fame and moved to Murfreesboro, Tennessee, where she lived until her death on March 17, 2005. Her last novel, *Three Hands for Scorpio,* was published by Tor Books in April, 2005.

RESEARCH AND ACTIVITIES
I. Wild Country
A. Corey sees Idaho as a frightening wilderness. Learn about the terrain, plant and animal life, and climate of Idaho. On a large sheet of paper, draw or paint an Idaho landscape based on your research. Note the season reflected in your drawing, and include some of the plants and animals mentioned in the novel.

B. Imagine you have arrived at Uncle Jasper's ranch and are looking out across the wilderness. Do you feel happy or sad, excited or frightened? What would you like to do? Write a letter to a friend or family member describing your arrival in Idaho.

C. Learn more about horses. Who brought horses to the Americas? What is a five-finger Appaloosa? In the character and costume of a 1960s Idaho rancher, a Native American, or a modern-day horse breeder, give a short oral presentation about the Appaloosa or another horse breed, its history and, if appropriate, its modern-day uses.

D. Plan an Idaho vacation inspired by *Fur Magic*. Travel along the Nez Perce National Historic Trail, camp in the Salmon-Challis National Forest, explore the Hagerman Fossil Beds National Monument, or visit a Native American reservation or museum. Write to an appropriate Chamber of Commerce, tourism bureau or other agency for more information. Create a trip itinerary including means of travel, lodging and dining spots, and key places to visit. Decorate a folder to hold your itinerary, maps, and other materials.

II. Native America

A. Go to the library or online to learn more about the Nez Perce tribe. Write a short report about the history, culture and customs of the Nez Perce based on your research.

B. Find out more about a notable Native American individual or group, such as Sacajawea, Squanto, or the Navajo code whisperers of World War II. Create a short oral presentation describing the life and contribution of this person or group. Design a monument commemorating this contribution to display in your home or classroom.

C. Learn more about Native American myths and legends. Prepare a dramatized version of one or two selected tales to perform in costume. Or create a mural or cartoon-style illustrated strip depicting key elements of the story. Discuss whether the legends you have researched remind you of stories from your own culture.

D. Based on your reading of *Fur Magic,* sculpt, draw or paint an image of the Changer. Then, go to the library to find books that include other Native American tales featuring this character. Compare your drawing to these book illustrations. Make a list of tribes that include a Trickster or Changer character in their mythology and the form or forms it takes for each tribe.

E. For Native American's, dreams can have powerful significance. Learn more about dreams in Native American culture. Then, create a survey to learn what your friends, classmates, or family members think of dreams. Are their thoughts similar to the Native American understanding of dreams? Compile your findings in a short report.

F. Go to the library or online to find instructions for making a Native American "dream catcher" and learn its purpose. Using sticks, colored string, feathers and/or other craft materials, make a dream catcher for your bedroom.

III. Changing and Belonging

A. Cory feels like an outsider in Idaho. In the character of Cory, write a journal entry describing your feelings. Or, in the character of Uncle Jasper, write a letter to Cory's father explaining your concerns about Cory and his adjustment to ranching life.

B. Write a short story about a time when you felt like an outsider, how and if you were able to fit in, and the people or experiences which helped you adjust.

C. In the novel, the author describes how the human Cory interprets or understands his beaver shape—he seems to be both inside and outside this form at the same time. Imagine that you have been magically transformed into an animal of your choice. Write an essay describing how you feel in your new body, the things you can and cannot do, and the way your human perceptions of the world have changed by experiencing in this new shape.

D. Role-play a scene in which Cory thanks Uncle Jasper or Black Elk for the lessons he has learned in Idaho. And/or act out a reunion between Cory and his father at the end of the summer. What new self-knowledge might Cory want to share? What changes might father, Uncle Jasper or Black Elk observe in Cory? With friends or classmates, take turns playing the different roles.

DISCUSSION QUESTIONS

1. What frightens Cory Alder in the beginning of *Fur Magic*? List the ways in which he feels like an outsider on Uncle Jasper's ranch. How might the events which brought Cory to Idaho be related to his difficult feelings?

2. What is Uncle Jasper's true relationship to Cory? How does Cory feel about Uncle Jasper? How does he think Uncle Jasper feels about him?

3. In the "Strong Medicine" chapter, what does Cory break and what does he do with these objects? What images does Cory see afterward? Is this a dream?

4. What does Black Elk insist that Cory do with the medicine bag? Could there be more than one reason for Black Elk's insistence? Explain your answer.

5. Into what animal is Cory transformed? Is he an ordinary version of this animal?

6. When Cory-Yellow Shell is captured by the minks, what does he recall Uncle Jasper saying about medicine dreams? How are they different from other dreams?

7. How are Cory's and Yellow Shell's thoughts intertwined? Why do you think this occurs? As their journey continues, how does this intertwining change? Cite examples from the novel.

8. Otter explains that, "There would come a day—all the medicine makers said it . . . that the world *would* turn over, when nothing would be as it now was. And all that was safe and sure would be swept away, and all that was straight would become crooked, all that was light would be dark." How does Yellow Shell understand these words? How might the otter's words be understood in terms of Cory's experience in Idaho and in his medicine dream world?

9. What roles do minks, otters, crows, and other animals from the dream portion of *Fur Magic* play? What role does the Changer play? Are the animals and the Changer good or bad characters? Explain.

10. What do the otters, eagles and Raven tell Yellow Shell to send him on his journey? Does Yellow Shell "already know" his mission before the animals tell him of it? Why might he know this?

11. What is Cory-Yellow Shell's reaction to the Changer? What bargain does Cory strike with the Changer? Does the result of the bargain frighten him? Why or why not?

12. Who are the People? What plan does the Changer describe to Cory and what will happen to the People as a result? Can his words be understood in any real-world terms, such as a description of the plight of the Native Americans or of the changing landscape of America in general?

13. What strength does Corey find to steal the medicine bag? What happens to Cory's form when he takes the bag?

14. What happens to the medicine bag as the story draws to a close? How does Cory find himself back at camp? What does Black Elk say has happened to the world? Has the world changed for Cory?

15. As Black Elk observes, dreaming has great significance for Native Americans. Do you believe dreams have meaning in modern life? Have you ever had a dream which seemed particularly significant to you? Describe this dream.

16. What has Corey's fantastic journey back to ancient Native American times taught him about fear and belonging? How has it changed his sense of himself in the present day and affected the way he can now approach his life with Uncle Jasper?